Forbidden Sweetness . . .

"Fear, my lord?"

"Yes. I fear I am losing you."

"That would imply you had me."

His head snapped in her direction. He pulled in on the reins. Standard snorted in alarm. Horse and gig halted in the middle of the empty road.

Turning to look her in the eyes, Philip demanded, "Did I not? Not even a little?" He looked at her, and kept on looking, his gaze delving, the road, the horse forgotten.

"You belong to another," she said, heart aching, unable to continue meeting his gaze.

With a gloved knuckle he raised her chin, insistent. "Do you feel nothing for me? I must know, for I am hopelessly in love, you see."

She could see. Love warmed his eyes and softened his lips. The onslaught of his eyes laid her bare, no chance of hiding her feelings.

He kissed her. She let him. She had yearned for this. Longing for him had gnawed at her soul. In kissing her, he filled the horrible aching hunger within. If only for this instant, the warm bond of their lips made a whole of two halves. Her lips were the flower, and he the bee, seeking nectar. Sweet, this kiss. Dangerous . . .

Coming next month

COUNTERFEIT KISSES
by Sandra Heath

Sir Gareth Carew was quite smitten by the attentions of London's lovely new arrival–until he recognized the charmer as Susannah Leighton, the woman who blamed him for the loss of her family's fortune. But can he win back her trust– and her love?

0-451-20022-5/$4.99

BURIED SECRETS
by Anne Barbour
"One of my favorite authors."–Mary Balogh

Love was for poets. Marriage was for fools. That was pretty much the philosophy of dashing rake Christopher Culver– until a scandalous spinster named Gillian Tate aroused his curiosity...and captured his heart.

0-451-20023-3/$4.99

THE NABOB'S DAUGHTER
by Dawn Lindsey

Anjelie Cantrell was the most sought-after heiress in Jamaica–and the most infuriating. Lord Chance is afraid the girl is more interested in mischief than marriage. That is, until their hearts were shipwrecked...

0-451-20045-4/$4.99

Breach
of
Promise

Elisabeth Fairchild

A SIGNET BOOK

SIGNET
Published by New American Library, a division of
Penguin Putnam Inc., 375 Hudson Street,
New York, New York 10014, U.S.A.
Penguin Books Ltd, 27 Wrights Lane,
London W8 5TZ, England
Penguin Books Australia Ltd, Ringwood,
Victoria, Australia
Penguin Books Canada Ltd, 10 Alcorn Avenue,
Toronto, Ontario, Canada M4V 3B2
Penguin Books (N.Z.) Ltd, 182–190 Wairau Road,
Auckland 10, New Zealand

Penguin Books Ltd, Registered Offices:
Harmondsworth, Middlesex, England

First published by Signet, an imprint of New American Library,
a division of Penguin Putnam Inc.

First Printing, April 2000
10 9 8 7 6 5 4 3 2 1

Chapter One

He sat the dun gelding, midway on the curving High Street, legs aching, chest tight, head throbbing. The memory of the rhythm of Standard's steady lope still beat in the muscles of buttocks and thighs, in the sore clench of his calves, in the very bones of his back.

A flock of swifts darted with rapid, audible wingbeats to roost beneath the stone arches of the village marketplace, flitting black silhouettes against the sun. It was time he roosted, too. He had kept a punishing pace for three days now, few stops along the way, riding blindly, no thought for food or sleep, or where he was going, until the sun lit golden the finialed outline of a church tower against the flat-topped darkness of a limestone escarpment, and Standard, winded and blowing, dropped to a walk and then a halt, and refused to go farther.

A long way the two of them had come, through an unfamiliar, gently rolling countryside dotted with well-tended fields and farms. Sheep and cattle grazed in emerald green pastures bordered by drystone walls rising like dragon's backs, topstones standing on end like loose scales. He had been blind to the beauty, deaf to the whistling call of the curlew, unaware of the sweet, clematis-scented caress of the breeze. And like the pounding of the horse's hoofbeats, so too had pounded his anger, nay it was a rage seethed in his veins. Nothing reached him, nothing touched him, until Chipping Campden.

The place glowed the color of honey, of cider, of a fizzing, pale champagne. The sun hung like a golden bauble, shedding yellowed afternoon light and shadow on the black-timbered Shakespearean temper of a thatch- and slate-roofed town dozing in unruffled prosperity. The beauty comforted him, quieting the fire of his anger. He had begun to believe all beauty slipped from his life with the loss of Lavinia—his ideal of her, at any rate—and yet here it was, staring him in the face, waiting to be noticed.

"I require lodgings," he told the tapman at the Red Lion, who served him a dram with the curious guardedness of a local to a stranger. Those gathered in the pub pretended unsuccessfully not to notice a stranger in their midst.

"We've rooms above, if you please, sir, or the Noel Arms is just up the High Street," the tapman suggested.

"Not an inn," Philip said with decided distaste. "I mean to stay awhile. A fortnight. Maybe two."

The tapman winked, his lips curling in a sly smile. "It's Mrs. Stott's honey house you'll be needin' to see."

Brows and murmurs rose up and down the bar.

"It is not a brothel I am in need of," Philip said dryly.

Two of the patrons stifled chuckles in the depths of their tankards.

A gleam lit the tapman's eyes. "Nor have we one in the neighborhood to send you to, sir."

Philip Randall Chalmondeley, Marquess of Chalmodeley and Earl of Rockforth, eyed him coolly, sensing himself the butt of some private joke. It was a role he seemed destined to play of late.

Curiosity aroused—they could play him for no

greater fool than he had already proved himself—he asked, "Where might I find this Mrs. Stott?"

Susan did not like to see an unknown gentleman standing on her step, hat in hand, windblown hair fired to a golden shimmer by the sun, shoulders stooped that he might see in a doorway built for a shorter people four hundred years gone.

She had grown wary of strangers, and the sheer glowing size of this lean fellow with stubbled jaw and red-rimmed eyes chased all breath from her throat, and froze her hand on the unsteady support of the door.

"Mrs. Stott?"

She frowned, disliking him immediately for addressing her as such. "I am Miss Susan Fairford," she said brusquely.

With distant green eyes he examined her, their color cool, weary, like treetops in a lazy breeze, his voice cool too, no attempt to engage her with smiles or pleasantries. "May I speak to Mrs. Stott? The tapman at the Lion sent me."

Burdock? Timothy Burdock's involvement did nothing to recommend a stranger who had not the manners to so much as introduce himself. And yet, she could not take her eyes off him.

He was not handsome so much as physically self-possessed, his every muscle poised to do his bidding, no gangly awkwardness in him, no annoying affectation of a walking stick needed to assist him in perambulation. He held his head proudly, like a stallion does, nose to the wind. He stood, weight evenly balanced. A man not easily swayed. And yet, she distrusted him from the start.

"To what purpose?" she asked.

A trace of irritation, like a bird in flight, flickered in those tired eyes. "She has a house to lease, furnished, with a garden?"

There was urgency to the question, and yet she took her time in answering. She had hoped for a well-to-do Cit's family escaping London's summer stench, or a high-ranking officer in the navy, temporarily grounded. She had advertised in all of the right newspapers and broadsheets in hopes of luring them to the heart of the Cotswolds.

This fellow had not the look of a family man. His complexion, while weathered, was not the tanned leather she expected in a seaman. His mud-spattered boots were of fine leather, the fabric of his waistcoat an expensive kerseymere in fashionable green. A gold watch fob draped heavy across his ribs. He carried just as heavily, an air of exhausted desperation. It worried her. A debt-ridden dandy who had gambled away his quarterly allowance and now chose to escape his creditors in the country was the last thing she needed.

"I know the house," she admitted with reluctance.

"I should like to see it." He began to lose patience.

"You bring a wife, sir? Children? It is a large house."

He laughed, a harsh bark of sound. The bloodshot eyes showed sudden heat, as though he found her suggestion offensive. "No wife," he said, each word crisply definitive. "No children. Nor any intended for the role. Nor do I foresee entertaining noisy hunting or racing parties. I would use gently this house of Mrs. Stott's."

He had the condescending air of a man accustomed to getting his way. It annoyed her, but it was not reason enough to reject him as tenant. She reached for her shawl, a lantern and the jingling key ring.

"I will show you."

The unwelcoming Miss Fairford stepped from the shadowed cottage doorway into the golden promise of a sunset that lit every strand of her hair as if with flame. A gold and bronze conflagration of stray curls fought the severe confinement of twisted braids, a defiant burn cooled by the cinnamon-dusted cream of her complexion.

Philip wondered briefly what such hair would look like unbound. Would it fall in untamed waves across the rose-tipped peaks of her breasts—as Lavinia's had? The curtains swayed in the window of the cottage next door. A woman peered out at them. He shoved aside the thought.

Miss Fairford regarded him with ill-concealed contempt, as if she knew his thoughts, his shame.

"In a hurry to get here, sir? Your horse is winded—lathered." Her gaze strayed, changed, pity there as she reached past him to stroke Standard's sweat-stained shoulder.

She smelled like spiced cake: cinnamon, cloves, honey. He caught scent of her hair as he turned with her toward the horse. Standard's familiar stink of sweat and leather overwhelmed her sweetness. Philip imagined he smelled the same. Scratching the sweet spot at the base of the dun's ear, he murmured, "In a blind rush to be off, weren't we, old man?"

"We'd best walk the poor beast." She flung the rebuke as lightly as the shawl she draped about her shoulders and catching up the unlit lantern led the way.

"Is there a place for him?" he asked, concerned too late for the animal. It was not himself alone he had thrown so wildly upon the world.

Copper-colored lashes, like her hair, made her eyes look all the bluer when they widened. Her lips twitched, as if he said something that amused her, something that left him a little contemptible in her eyes. "Timothy Burdock told you nothing about the house, now did he?"

He was all too worthy of contempt, of course, but to find it in a stranger's eyes unsettled him.

"Burdock said only that it was likely the single

house in the neighborhood to suit me, and Mrs. Stott keen to lease it."

She shivered, drawing the woolen shawl closer about her shoulders. It was knobby in texture, knitted in the same honeyed colors of the local stone. She looked a part of the place, he decided, as if she sprang from the elements, a perfect blend of earth, rock, fire and water.

A tempting beauty he might have considered her at any other time in his life. Today he considered her the enemy, a creature to beware.

Down a lane she led him, hips swaying dangerously, an occasional distrustful blue-eyed glance thrown over her shoulder, as if she knew the lure of her derriere, as if she resented the unintentional drift of his gaze.

"Will you wait here while I stop in a moment?" She paused at the gate before an ivy-draped, thatched cottage, rose garden in full bloom. Flaming curls drifted across her forehead in the breeze, kissing her cheek.

He stood with Standard by the gate, expecting her to emerge with the missing Mrs. Stott, the smell of lamb chop and browning bread mingled with the sweet perfume of drifted rose petals. He could not help but think of home. The Maiden's Blush had been in full bloom. Perfect for a wedding, and he perfectly ready to be wed. It had been the reason for this journey that was not at all anticipated.

A bee buzzed by his ear, and with it the sound of voices from the window of the cottage, a woman speaking, and he not meant to hear. "I know you've no wish to take him there alone, Susie, my dear. Not fitting."

He could hear no more than the murmur of a voice he knew already as Miss Fairford's, then the woman again. "I've supper on the hob, lass, and Jerry due any minute. Shall I send the lads with you?"

It seemed she should, for when Miss Fairford appeared she was followed by two dark-haired boys. He guessed their ages at about eight and ten. They were introduced to him as David and Henry, and she gave into the eldest boy's care the ring of keys.

With the feeling he was being watched, he looked away from the boys to find their mother standing at the window, peering out at them, no more than an impression of graying hair and jowled chin.

"Run ahead now," Miss Fairford told the boys. "Open the door, bring in a bit of firewood for the downstairs' hearth, and see to it there is fresh pumped water for the horse."

"Yes, Miss Fairford," they agreed in unison, and darted ahead along the lane, disappearing as they rounded a bend. Their mother's face disappeared from the window.

They were alone again, and mutually uneasy in said state, the uneasiness of strangers, man and woman, without sufficient knowledge or introduction. Darting quick, measuring glances at each other, they followed the route the boys had taken, alongside a chuckling stream, away from the cheek-by-jowl coziness of the houses near the High Street, sunlight flickering through beech tree and oak, leaves dancing a gilded green in the evening breeze.

"I do not know your name, sir." She made the first attempt to ease the tension. "Nor where you hail from."

He hesitated, unprepared, unwilling to be known for the stupid fool he was. Eyes drawn to the glowing faux gold of the houses they passed, he clicked his heels together, bowed with courtly grace and cloaked himself in a lie. "Philip Randall Stone of . . . Dorset. At your service. I do apologize, Miss Fairford. I should have introduced myself immediately."

Susan noticed that he gave county rather than town as his residence, and that he hesitated in revealing

even that much. She had known another gentleman
who began the same uncertain way. A liar. She hated
liars. She wondered if there was any truth to Philip
Randall Stone, of Dorset.

The dun nickered, blew its nose gustily and
mouthed the bit. An animal of excellent conformation.
He must have cost Mr. Stone a pretty penny. Had the
man money, or only the pretense of it?

Determined to know more, determined not to believe a word he said until it was proven, she asked, "Is
it business or pleasure brings you to Gloucestershire?"

"The road brings me," he said, and she could not
tell if the shadow that crossed his features was pique,
or no more than the gloom of the trees. "The quiet
beauty of this place made me stop. I am in need of a
bit of quiet—a place to think." He rubbed at the faint
pucker between fair brows.

She wondered what worried him.

They reached the low, humpbacked stone bridge,
their footsteps and the clop of the dun's hooves echoing from the water below. Nestled in a little wilderness
on the far side of the stream, the imposing stone gateway loomed. The black wrought iron gate stood ajar.
It gave her a pang every time she passed it these days.
Through the alders three familiar gabled rooftops
emerged, a glow of honey gold stone on the familiar
peaked brows.

"Fairford Manor," she said with forced cheer-
fulness. "Do you like the look of it?"

They could not have seen it in better light. It had
the look of a place enchanted, half asleep in the waning sun, awaiting the wave of a wand, or the heat of
a prince's kiss.

"Your house?" he asked, surprised, and she realized
she could not take her eyes from his mouth when he
spoke—firm lips, shapely. A liar's mouth? "But it is
charming," those lips said. "Are we to be neighbors,
then, if I take Mrs. Stott's property?"

Did his gaze warm, or was it the reflected glow of the sun?

"There is no Mrs. Stott, Mr. Stone." The words came harsher, more heated than she meant to voice them.

His eyes, his features, took on a glacial chill.

She sighed and modified her tone. "Never was. This is the property in question."

Remaining quiet for a long, thoughtful moment, he defused the growing tension between them and changed the subject by asking calmly, "What is this fine honey-colored stone with which you build here?"

She collected her thoughts, her breath, her emotions. "And what part of Dorset are you from, sir, with a name like Stone, if you do not know prime oolite when you see it?"

He turned, his gaze cool, shadowed as a forest, blue rings beneath his eyes. From dissolute lifestyle or sleeplessness? His lips twitched. She had amused him with the question.

"Forgive my ignorance. I hail from the coast," he admitted. "We build in gray granite there."

She wondered where on the coast—Weymouth? Bournemouth? Lyme Regis?

They emerged from the trees. Blank-faced, the house stared at them, windows dark. She did not like to see the weeds taking over the courtyard, bird's nests trailing from the eaves.

"Oolite?" he murmured. "Egg stone?"

He translated from the Greek. No mindless dandy here—a man of letters.

She went to the nearest courtyard wall and finding a bit of broken limestone shed one glove and rubbed the tip of her finger against the raw surface. "The local freemasons call it roestone. You see, it is made up of tiny round bits."

He bared his hand, and held it out, that she might brush the round bits from her fingertips into his palm.

The horse crowded them briefly, bumping his master's arm. Mr. Stone's outstretched fingers brushed past hers, grazed, like a falling leaf, across her breast, alarming her every sensibility, the sensation at once pleasantly arousing and horribly shaming.

She gasped, cheeks feverish as she backed away, appalled.

He stepped back as well, increasing the distance between them with a quick, "I do beg your pardon."

It crossed her mind, insensibly, that he had heard rumors of her at the Lion, that he meant to take advantage, here, in her own home, as dusk descended. That flash of indignant fear must have expressed itself in her eyes, for he turned away abruptly, green eyes more remote than ever, to gently scold the horse, even as he stroked the dun's nose. The gentleness of his caress unnerved her, visually echoing the stray touch that had aroused her nipples to an uncomfortable, vigilant erectness, and her pulse to a racing throb.

"Great clumsy brute," he murmured, voice as silken as his touch. "Have you no idea how to behave in the presence of a lady? Forgive him, Miss Fairford."

He bent to touch the stone rather than look at her, rolling the grains he gathered between his fingertips. "Pray forgive me."

She took a deep breath, and pressed the flat of one hand to her throat, as if she could, by touch, slow the race of her pulse. "I understand the rock in some way contains coral," she said, her voice, at least, controlled and steady.

Interest caught, his eyes revealed again the depths of an exhaustion so deep she longed to say, "To bed with you, sir."

And yet, his curiosity was not too tired to ask, "Was this once ocean where we stand?"

She nodded. "Long ago."

"Why do you not still live here, little mermaid?" He waved at the house. She could hear faint embar-

rassment in the question, a sentiment that endeared
him to her.

She forced herself to smile, unwilling to allow emotion to overwhelm her. "It is too big a place for a
single mermaid alone. Too many servants required,
and funds to pay them."

"Ah!" His gaze held no pity. She would have hated
pity. She could not quite fathom what emotion registered there, but that some change overtook his features was undeniable.

"The stables." She pointed, unwilling to become,
too long, the focus of his attention. "Perhaps you
would like to water your horse? Have a look around?
The lads and I will bring some light into the house
unless you can see from the outset that Fairford is not
what you had in mind."

He chirruped to the horse, the dun lifting its head
to nuzzle his shoulder. He fingered the pale forelock,
stroked the velvety nose, expressing with his every
sleepy, gentle move and touch an unguarded affection
for the animal.

His gaze rose, sunlight hitting obliquely the green
of his eyes. "Will you show me your honey house?"
he asked with those captivating lips.

Her body responded with an unexpected wave of
heat. Her head, far more sensible than her body, re-
newed its suspicions of him, warning her not to be a
fool—not again.

"You know about the bees?" she asked.

Chapter Two

B *ees?* Bees, indeed!

Philip led Standard to the stables, berating himself for trusting the tapman, Burdock, and for repeating the name Burdock had cruelly given Miss Fairford's fine house.

Philip had assumed the odd moniker had something to do with the color of the stone. And yet, he could not chase from his mind the picture of her face when he said it. A hint of shock, then a flash of pained annoyance. She had the look of someone who had just been slapped when she calmly mentioned her bees.

From what little he knew of Burdock, and the none too gentlemanly reaction he had won from his patrons, Philip suspected, too late, he had other reasons entirely for calling her place a honey house.

Was Miss Fairford a fallen woman? Why had Burdock identified her as Mrs. Stott?

The ancient stables were snugly constructed and sensibly arranged, though built on far smaller proportions than that to which he was accustomed. Philip thought briefly about sending for his carriage and four, then dismissed the notion, pleased with the idea of anonymity, intrigued by the vision of Mr. Stone, simple country squire, tooling along in a one-horse gig.

Yes, that suited his mood. The simple life. A simple society. No promises made, none to keep.

His every move slowed by exhaustion, he watered Standard, stripped him of saddle and bridle, gave him a cursory rubdown, and loosed him to graze in the walled meadow beside the stables. The sun had sunk behind the trees when he turned again to the house. It was no longer the brick that glowed, but Tudor windows—arched-headed—an attractive architectural touch. Mr. Stone would do well here on his repairing lease, very well indeed, barring further verbal blunders.

He opened the door as if it were already his, and stepped into the Great Hall, a chill, echoing space, alive with dark corners despite the fire glowing on the hearth. Too few candles for his taste. He would not have a true measure of the place until morning and the light of day, and yet he felt it had begun recklessly, why not end it in the same manner?

Miss Fairford rose from where she knelt by the hearth, sparks flying, bellows in hands, a fire sprite taking human form, the blaze of her hair fresh revelation against the ghostly backdrop of dustcovered furniture. He resented her effect on him, resented the idea that any woman might move him again with beauty, promises and lies. He had no desire to be troubled by desire.

"I shall require servants," he said harshly.

Head cocked, she adjusted the hang of her shawl and rubbed a bit of ash from the palms of her gloves, the faint, annoying hint of contempt returning to her gaze. "You have yet to see the house, Mr. Stone."

"Yes." He forced a smile, amending his tone. "*Should* I require servants, are there locals I might hire? Or must I send to Gloucester for them?"

She took up her lamp and set off through the darkly paneled archway at the far end of the room, light and shadow moving across the bas relief faces staring down at them in just such a way that it seemed heads turned, watching her glowing passage as closely as he did.

"That would depend, Mr. Stone. How many ser-

vants you had in mind, and how much you care to
endear yourself locally."

"A small staff, rudimentary." His tired voice echoed
from the ceilings as he followed her through the chill,
stone-floored buttery, into the kitchen, copper pots
gleaming, into the faint scent of cinnamon.

Was it she who smelled so edible? Or merely the
ghosts of past cookery?

"A cook?" she suggested.

Servants. They spoke of servants.

"A spit tender and a pastry chef," he added wearily.

She held high the lamp within the dark nook of the
scullery, the light pleasing as it passed over her form,
fire reflected in fire when it touched her hair. "A scullery maid?"

"Better make it two."

As they examined the pantry and passed through
the housekeeper's chambers, he found his eyes drawn
continually to her hair, her face, the enticing curve at
the small of her back, as he added to the list: a butler,
valet, two or three footmen, a housekeeper, five
maids, a groom, two stable boys and a gardener or
two.

"Will it be enough?" She asked sarcastically, a dim-
ple peeping in her fair, freckled cheek, head tilted in
such a way he thought her an imp, laughing at him.
They made their way through an ill-lit room with window seats beneath arching glass that opened onto the
dusk-darkened garden, with the smell of damp earth
and the tune of crickets singing.

"What is this used for?" he asked, rather than respond to her goading.

She settled one knee on a window seat, tilting wide
the hinged window frame, face turned to the tarnished
silver of the sky, lamplight pooled at her feet. The
strained line of her back and shoulder moved him, as
nothing about her had moved him until now. He knew
it taxed her to offer him what had once been hers.

She breathed deep the night air, turning to him with features both starlit and wistful. "It *was* the nursery," she said with a sigh. "You may use it as you will."

Susan saw the house through fresh eyes in leading Mr. Stone up the stairs. She wondered what he thought as they trod the beautiful wood-floored chambers laid out long ago by her ancestor's ancestors, memories echoing as much as their footsteps.

As if he read her mind, he asked, "Were you born here?"

"Yes."

Her back ached. Her shoulders felt stiff. She did not bother to elaborate.

She walked him through the first-floor family apartments, bedchambers and withdrawing rooms. Here she had slept. And here the mother she had never known had died of smallpox when she was two, and her father in his sleep four years gone. Here were the rooms where her aunts and uncles, cousins and friends had stayed when they came for the funerals, the reading of the wills, and eventually for the wedding that should never have been. Most of them shunned her now that she no longer inhabited Fairford, now that she could no longer afford to entertain them in grand style.

Shame. She grew weary of the shame. Wasn't it Stott who should be shamed, not she?

She swung wide the door to an all-too-familiar stone-paved room with the heavy, gleaming wooden bath she had considered too large for the confines of her present cottage.

Here she had bathed in preparation for her wedding night. The view from dusk-dimmed windows read as clearly to her memory as if it were daylight.

"The bath," she said.

"You did not take it with you?"

The unfamiliar echoing timber of his voice in the

confined space reminded her that he was a stranger, with whom she walked virtually alone through the deserted house, Naomi's boys like quiet ghosts, lighting candles before them.

"As you see."

"And yet you seem well scrubbed." The green eyes warmed momentarily with humor, the captivating lips tilted upward in a smile, rendering him harmless.

In that instant she wanted to laugh with him, to like him without reservation. She wanted to trust him. It was her natural inclination to trust. How wearying to always suspect the worst of people—men in particular.

His face went cool again, distant.

"It was not the only tub in the house," she said. "Merely the largest. Wholly unsuitable for my current surroundings."

"You live, then, in the cottage on the High Street, not Mrs. Stott?"

Her lips parted on an explanation. She closed them again. He would find out soon enough from the local gossips.

"I do."

He could not imagine showing a stranger about his family holdings, as she did, with the intent that they should live there, even briefly. He blurted out a cut-off laugh. What had the Marquess of Chalmondeley and Earl of Rockforth done in showing Miss Lavinia Keck around Rockforth Hall but given tour to one who would be tenant?

What a fool he had been.

"Mr. Stone? Something amuses you?"

The unfamiliar name took á moment to register, but Miss Fairford's face by candlelight was becoming familiar indeed, contours gilded and shadow struck, her expression guarded and wary.

"My life, Miss Fairford. It is a farce of late."

He wanted to laugh again. Why in blazes had he

called himself Stone, of all things, if he could not re-member to respond to it? It occurred to him that he was turned to stone today—hard, resistant, able to withstand the weathering elements that rained down on him. He would not forget again.

"Do you wish to see the second floor?" she asked, poised to take the next flight of stairs, her hand curled around a newel post carved in the shape of a lamb. A pale hand, soft, the fingers rounded, something lamblike in it.

"Of course," he said, and followed the enticing sway of her hips to the next floor, completely unmoved by her movements. It was thus he had fallen prey to Lavinia, by way of her hips, and then her lips. Never again, he promised himself. He would look deeper into the heart and soul of every woman he met before he allowed himself to trust again, to love again.

It was strange for him, to imagine that Miss Fairford had slept in one of the bedchambers now to be his, to wonder if she had taken her first steps in the nursery below, to picture her playing in the second-floor long gallery, where the portraits of her ancestors still watched over the house.

"I can have them taken down," she offered. "Stored in the attic. You will want to bring in your own family portraits or wall hangings, should you decide to stay."

"No!" he protested, his voice too strong, too vehement, this loss of control unwanted evidence of his exhaustion. She did not understand his aversion to remembering. "I mean to be a tenant only briefly," he tried to explain politely. "A fortnight or two. I would not have you turn the place upside down for me."

"You mean to take Fairford, then?" she asked, hope in her eyes, the wary wall of her guarded features momentarily breached.

He lifted his gaze to the plaster-worked ceiling, a pattern of boxes within boxes. His eyelids, too heavy,

kept wanting to close out sight of them. There was
within him a niggling sense of guilt in taking a house
from a woman who wore the same name. "Yes," he
said. "I shall spend the night at the Noel Arms, and
with your permission, and the hiring of servants, take
possession before the week is out."

"Good!" she said, a brief, relieved brightening of
her features fading swiftly as her gaze swept the room,
settling on him with sudden shrewdness. "The place
is yours as soon as I see payment."

Chapter Three

"Payment." He frowned, rubbed his forehead and tried to concentrate his straying thoughts.

She wore a very businesslike expression, Miss Fairford, and he, exhausted, felt completely at sea. He had been in a mood to despise his money at the moment of his flight from Rockforth Hall, from Lavinia. It was the root of his troubles. As a result, he had raced away with no more than what he had in his pockets.

A few coins, no more.

A promissory note upon his bank would draw sufficient funds, of course, but a note in the name of Stone would yield no assets at all. There was no said account. To sign his real name would destroy his anonymity. What was a Mr. Stone to do?

Dover! Dover would handle it, without revealing his whereabouts, But, Dover was in London.

"I must ride to"—What was the nearest city where he might handle his finances? Cheltenham? Tewkesbury? Winchcombe? Surely he need not ride all the way to Gloucester?—"Cheltenham," he said decisively, "to see to a transfer to funds."

She frowned, the blue of her eyes surprised, even suspicious. He was unused to women regarding him with anything other than respect, coy flirtatiousness or bold-faced desire. Lavinia had fooled him into thinking she felt all three. This woman's searching gaze revealed nothing of the kind. Contempt she had shown him, and suspicion. Would her outlook change, he wondered, were he to announce himself by his true title?

He thought not.

Miss Fairford, it seemed, was a woman soured to men. He wondered what unworthy fellow had so spoiled her view of his sex.

"Will not our bank here in Campden do, Mr. Stone? Or if you would prefer to do business along one of the main coach roads, Evesham is far closer."

She was practical, helpful, his fairy-haired landlady, even in her distrust of him. He did not want her to dislike him, to hold him always skeptically at arm's length. Not if they were to conduct business together.

"Evesham? To the west?"

"Less than ten miles. Just beyond the Avon. An easy distance over good roads."

"Thank you, Miss Fairford. Evesham it is."

She worried about the money as she watched him ride into the darkness.

A distasteful preoccupation. But what was her life of late, but a constant struggle with pounds and pence?

She thanked David and Henry and sent them home.

Her hands shook as she went about the house, lamp in hand, dousing candles, extinguishing the light that had, briefly, brought alive to her, too fresh, too painful, the full scope of what she had once had and lost.

And for the moment she was saved by a stranger, a self-assured stranger who rode into Campden full of promises, much like the handsome stranger who had promised her love, happiness and a rosy future before he systematically destroyed all three.

Stott. She would not think of Stott. She had promised herself she would not allow him to possess her thoughts any longer. Not with doubts. Not with guilt. Not with anger. She would not allow the dreadful man to steal any more from her than he had already taken.

She paused on the threshold of her old bedchamber, drawn to the high, wide, comfortable bed, moved to fling back the dustcovers, unveiling the massive, carved cherry bedposts, the aging damask bed hangings in shades of chestnut, brick brown and a sea green that made her think of Mr. Stone's distant gaze.

These, her treasured possessions, would fit in her tiny cottage no more than the big bathtub. She slept now in a bed that had once served her old housekeeper, Mrs. Tully—a large woman, recently deceased, who had left her imprint upon the sagging cloth webbing that had once held her feather mattress. Susan ran a hand up one of the carved bedposts. Her heart ached with longing for a bed that did not sink almost to the floor beneath her weight, for a mattress ticking that did not fold in upon her as she tossed and turned in the middle of the night.

Her old bed beckoned grandly, like a matron aunt, arms wide, on whose bosom she had wept more than once.

She gave in to desire. She had always been weak that way. Dustcovers folded away, she started a fire in the bedroom hearth, and set a kettle to heat water for the bath. Half the night was spent, and she with it, before she climbed at last beneath fresh-tucked linen, her hair still damp from her indulgence, her skin scented of the rose petals she had squandered from the garden.

She thrilled to the almost forgotten luxury, her heart happy to see the familiar outline of her room in darkness, moonlight shedding an almost forgotten pattern on the Aubusson rug. She fell asleep smiling, dreaming herself mistress of Fairford again, free of care or want, or dangerous desires, heiress to her father's small fortune.

Philip did not sleep well. What man would? He was supposed to be wallowing in newly wedded bliss. He had not slept well since he had ridden away from Lavinia, whose bed he had hoped to share for a lifetime. Now, at the Noel Arms, he had only rage, pain, exhaustion and a keen sense of betrayal to cling to.

He swore to himself he would not think of her, would not think of their final encounter. He could fix his mind on nothing else.

Pacing did not distract him. Counting sheep was pointless. He listened to the sounds of the Noel Arms settling. The street below stilled, the stars climbed the sky, and still he found no rest, no peace. He had come to this place for both.

Was his flight a failure? He had made a mad dash to escape harsh reality, yet the ugly truths he wanted neither to confront or believe followed him. Like a dog, tail tucked, he had run away to lick his wounds—halfway across England.

And by God, why not?

Why should he be the one to clean up the wedding day's messy aftermath?

He rose from the bed for the umpteenth time, and standing at the window stared out at the bell-towered town hall across the street, beside it the steeply gabled marketplace. A quiet place, a pretty place, even by moonlight.

He thought of Miss Fairford, of the bright glow of her hair, of the contemptuous glow in her eyes. Why should she regard him so when she knew nothing of him? He had accepted her silent scorn as his due. But was it? Yes, he admitted with a sigh. Lavinia had seen to that—clever, devious strumpet.

He turned from the view of the moonlit village to regard the rumpled, uninviting bed. *Sleep.* He needed sleep. He could not stay here forever, he knew that. He would have to go back, to deal with promises breached and promises undone.

But not right away.

*   *   *

He dozed, then rose early, the dew still wet upon the grass when he and Standard set out for Evesham, and a bank to finance his golden idyll.

He decided before they had gone two steps that it made sense to take another look at the place he meant to inhabit, clear-eyed, clear-headed—by the light of day. And so he rode from the Noel Arms to Miss Fairford's honey house.

The beeches were alive with the flutter of wings, the happy twittering of finches and sparrows, the *chuck-tchack* of a warbler, the ringing *pink pink* of the chaffinch. Small silver blue butterflies hung about the margins of the road. So different from home. So much more color here. The stream he and the horse must cross by way of the humpback bridge chortled and splashed, and yet he missed the constant hushing roar of the ocean, the bluster of a ceaseless wind, the shrill keening of gulls.

Behind the screen of gently rustling alders Fairford proved no less beautiful by morning light than it had been in the golden glory of sunset. Strange how he thought at once of the shaped shrubbery that added distinction to the stalwart Jacobean face of Rockforth Hall and wondered if he ought not leap into the saddle and head south.

There was a delicate purpling quality to this oolite stone in the shadows. Philip thought of coral beaches and eyes as blue as the sea on a sunny day. He dismounted, lashing Standard to the ball-topped post near the doorstep. With a pleased eye he walked the perimeter of the house. Rows of humming straw beehives sat halfway beneath the trees on the south front. Honey houses, not house. He skirted them judiciously, ending where he had started, at the front door.

It was a fine manor. Lovelier by daylight than he had expected. He could be very comfortable here for a fortnight or two.

Sure it would be locked, he yet gave the door latch

a press, amazed to feel it give way, the door swinging wide with a slight wail of hinges. Country ways he knew well enough. Many where he came from saw little reason to lock their doors against neighbors they trusted like family.

He had trusted—left the door to his heart unlocked, welcomed thieves to his bosom.

He hesitated, leaned in the doorway, cleared his throat and called out, "Haloo, anybody home?"

No sound met his ear but the echo of his own words, no scent found his nose but a faint whiff of last night's beeswax candles. He stepped inside the Great Hall, drinking in the sight of it in daylight, a different picture entirely from the one painted by candlelight. The faces carved in the screen at the far end of the wall were not alive in the morning light, merely beautifully decorative, as wooden-headed as he felt himself this morning after his restless night.

The room looked dustier by day, the windows in need of a scrubbing, cobwebs gathering in corners. And yet it was an uncluttered place, furniture well covered, the walls and paneling sound, no sign of wood rot or leaking roof. He would, of course, have to check the upstairs to be sure.

Through the buttery, kitchen, scullery and pantry he traipsed, footsteps echoing. He felt the intruder here without Miss Fairford to lead the way. The stairs creaked as he mounted them. Above, the beams groaned. A chill struck him, the ghost of a draft running chill fingers through his hair. Portraits looked down on him in the paneled stairwell—Miss Fairford's erstwhile relatives, her chin in one, her fiery hair and freckles recorded in several, her blue eyes everywhere.

The first floor smelled vaguely of roses, an elusive sweetness that brought the young woman again to mind. She was a red rose if ever there was one. Not at all like Lavinia's flaxen fairness and peaches-and-cream complexion.

Had Miss Fairford worn the scent of roses? No, cinnamon. The smell of oranges had won him before. He would never eat the fruit again.

With an eye to ceiling and floor, he walked the withdrawing rooms and bedchambers, the perfume of roses stronger, explanation to be seen in an open window that overlooked the garden. He twitched back a dust-cover or two, studying the available furniture. He liked the feel of the place, the colors and textures in the draperies, wall hangings and rugs. He could see himself comfortable here, torn spirit mending.

He could not decide which of the bedchambers to make his own, never expected to open the door of the second he explored to reveal a rumpled bed, and in it a sleeping maiden, hair spread across the pillow like shimmering flame.

"Oh, no!" he blurted without thinking. It would have been far wiser had he simply backed out of the room.

His voice roused her. She rose, leggy as a startled fawn, shaking the curtain of hair from her eyes, clutching the bedclothes to her breast to peer at him from the bedcurtains. She was bare-shouldered, but for a dusting of cinnamon-colored freckles. He imagined all of her bare, cinnamon-dusted beneath the sheets.

"Good God! What do you do here?"

Her outrage came as no surprise. With her rose his memory of Lavinia, crying out in exactly the same words.

He inhaled abruptly, murmured, "Do forgive me!" and backed out of the room, closing the door behind him as swiftly as he had opened it.

Heart racing, he sank against the carved oak with a muffled oath, eyes closed, unable to close his mind to the memory of another flash of bare skin swiftly covered, bedclothes flying, shocked expressions, yelps of dismay.

What fiend was Fate to machinate a second untimely entrance into a young woman's most private chamber when he was not wanted—not wanted at all?

"Mr. Stone?"

Her voice sounded more angry than frightened from the far side of the door. He supposed he had just spoiled all chance at tenanting the house.

"Miss Fairford. I do beg your pardon. I had no idea—"

"What the devil do you mean, sir, walking in on me like that? How did you get in?"

He could hear the sound of a scurry, and imagined her diving for clothing, bed linens clutched about her like a Roman toga.

He played the fool—again—he played the fool.

"I came to see the place by daylight. The door was unlocked. I began to think of the place as mine already. It never occurred to me you might be here."

The doorway across the corridor drew his gaze. Through it he could see the edge of the polished wooden tub, and beside it a chair across the back of which hung what looked like neatly folded clothing. He stepped closer.

Her clothes—and she in desperate need of them.

"You will leave now, Mr. Stone," she called forcefully. He knew she must stand, wrapped in sheets, copper curls curtained about her shoulders, wishing him to the very devil.

He determined to right the situation as much as he could.

"Mr. Stone?" she called when he did not answer.

He lifted the chair, legs scraping the stone floor with pained screeches.

"What are you doing, Mr. Stone?" The note of desperation had returned.

"Rearranging the furniture, Miss Fairford," he called back to her.

With as much haste as he could muster lugging about heavy oak, he carried the chair, clothing and all, to her doorway, and settled it with a thump where she would see it as soon as she came out.

"I beg you will leave, Mr. Stone."

She sounded remarkably sure of herself, given the situation. He admired her for that.

"On my way now, Miss Fairford," he assured her, and clattered downstairs and into the courtyard, where, much bemused, he took a turn or two, gravel crunching, debating whether to mount Standard and ride away at once, or remain and determine if she might forgive him—at least enough to hold fast to her agreement to lease the house to him.

He made it as far as the humpbacked bridge before he forced himself to stop with the thought that he could not run away from every little trouble in life, no matter how embarrassing. He staked Standard to graze, therefore, and sat down at the bridge's peak, legs dangling, to wait.

She was surprised to see him sitting in dappled sunshine, flipping pebbles into the stream—waiting for her.

Her cheeks heated afresh. What did one say to a stranger who had seen one leap naked from bed?

She ought never to have placed herself in such a vulnerable position, ought not to lease him Fairford, ought to wait for the family she had envisioned.

He rose, dusting off the palms of his gloves and the seat of his doeskin britches, all too tall, entirely too young and physically fit to suit her. All she could think about was bare skin, and how quickly she had covered it. How much had he seen? How badly they had started the day. How little she wanted to face him.

"I would apologize again," he began, and the look on his face was one of perfect contrition, rather than the lewd brashness it might have been. "It was wholly inappropriate for me to walk into your property without permission or escort."

His tone was coolly unemotional. His green eyes were as distant as ever they had been—his manner somewhat startling. She had begun to believe him another Mr. Stott, who would have smiled at her endearingly, and done his best to sway her with suggestive words, a jest or two, and seductive glances. Not Mr. Stone.

He studied his boots, eyes drawn briefly, as were hers, to the buzzing shimmer of a black-barred dragonfly—no, there were two, linked in mating, hovering between them—all too untimely.

Mr. Stone scowled and turned away, the scrunch of his boots frightening the united insects to safety under the bridge.

"I will understand entirely if you no longer feel comfortable leasing me the place."

He could not look at her.

Mr. Stott would have alluded to the happy insects with winning smiles, and falsely suggested he wished he might take on the burden of a wife so skillfully.

Mr. Stone was not a Mr. Stott.

"It was kind of you . . . the chair . . . my clothes," she said.

Still he would not look at her.

"Least I could do. Unfortunate circumstances," he said.

"As to our agreement . . ." She must think sensibly, she reminded herself. She must have income or lose the house altogether. "I would not renege on our business in a foolish pique, sir."

That brought his head up, his eyes locking briefly on hers. "Good!"

She read a pleased sort of surprise in his gaze, and curiosity, as if her response startled and intrigued him.

Her turn to look away. "I ought never to have stayed at the house once it was promised to you," she said.

"But—"

She would not allow him to go on. "This sort of . . . unfortunate circumstance will, of course, never happen again."

"Of course," he agreed. He caught up his horse, and as he swung into the saddle said, "It is a lovely house . . . a particularly lovely bath. I, too, would have wanted to enjoy them one last time."

A trifle alarmed by his perceptiveness, by the feeling that those remote green eyes took in far more than she had heretofore credited them with, she watched him ride away, wondering once again what brought such a man to Chipping Campden with no more upon his person than the exceptionally fine clothes upon his remarkably fine figure.

Chapter Four

Mr. Buttersby, the manager of the bank in Evesham, was more than happy to serve his lordship, whose extensive holdings in Devon and Cornwall he had some idea of—it would be easy enough to verify what exactly they entailed. The Earl of Rockforth, Marquis of Chalmondeley's wealth went without question.

"You wish to keep private your business here, my lord?" Buttersby lowered his voice and looked about him, as if there lurked spies who would force him to tell. "But, of course," he agreed with a conspiratorial smile as oily as his name. "Your wish is my command, my lord."

"You will forward all queries and requests by way of Mr. Dover, my solicitor in London," Philip instructed. "He is the only one in my employ who knows my whereabouts."

"Just so, my lord."

"I am on a repairing lease, not financial, but of spirit, and wish to be known in the neighborhood only as Mr. Stone. You are the only one who knows otherwise. Can I trust you, Mr. Buttersby, to keep my secret?"

Philip gracefully slid several gold coins in the banker's direction.

Mr. Buttersby's eyes gleamed. "My lips are sealed, my lord."

Philip pocketed the rest of the coins he needed for

Miss Fairford, signed the paperwork for the account in his name, and turning to go, asked, "Is there a good tailor hereabouts, Mr. Buttersby? And do you know of anyone interested in selling or leasing a gig?"

Buttersby preened to be asked assistance in such personal matters.

"On the far side of the fruit market, my lord," he said. "Look for Mr. Perkins's shopfront. He is quite masterful with his needle. Serves the local squires."

"Thank you," Philip said. "But you must remember to address me hereafter as Mr. Stone."

"Yes, yes. Mr. Stone." Buttersby bobbed an obsequious bow. "I shall remember. Never fear."

Susan spent her morning talking to the local waits, searching out those looking for a position, wondering privately if she would ever see Mr. Stone again.

Word was out. Everywhere she went talk centered on the mysterious gentleman who had put up at the Noel Arms. Everywhere she went she was asked about him.

"Queer goings on up at Fairford last night," the blacksmith's sister was eager to tell the women who gathered at the bakery, little realizing that her shrill tone carried into the street outside the baker's window as strongly as the wonderful yeasty smell of fresh bread and sweet buns.

The gossip brought a bitter taste to Susan's mouth. She debated whether she ought to come back later. She despised gossip—refused to participate in it. Too often had it been turned against her.

"A strange dun horse was grazing in the paddock, and lamplight and candles enough that I was half convinced the place had caught fire," Mrs. Clark from down the road was quick to tell them. "Sent me brother over for a peek."

"Dun horse, did you say?" asked the squire's housekeeper. "Why, a pale horse was tethered by the door at Fairford early this morning. I caught a glimpse of the creature as I made my way into town for the posting of a letter to my sister."

They quieted as she came through the door, basket in hand.

"Is the gentleman from the Red Lion to take Fairford, Susan?" Miss Millie Burdock, the tapman's sister, asked, her face avid with the bright-eyed interest that only good gossip stirred.

"What is his name? Stone?"

"Where is he from?"

"What do you think of him?"

"A fine figure of a man, I have heard."

"Is he on the run from creditors?"

"He rides a well-bred dun horse, does he not?"

"What brings a young man of means to Campden Town?"

Like her bees, their busy buzz. She could not help but think what an agitated noise her marriage must have stirred. Had these familiar faces lit with just such glee when she had been the source of speculation?

"A loaf of rye, if you please," Susan directed the baker's wife.

"Come now, Susan, don't be purse-lipped," Millie said fretfully. "We would know summat of this stranger."

"My new tenant calls himself Mr. Stone, and he has indicated that he treasures his privacy, and stays here because he considers it a beautiful and quiet place. More than that I cannot tell you."

"Cannot, or will not?" snapped the baker's wife.

"I thank you for the bread," Susan said curtly, then left them—but not so fast she did not hear Mrs. Clark remark in dissatisfaction, "Was not Miss Fairford closemouthed?"

"Queer how she does always seem to be the one to convince young men to linger," Millie said spitefully.

Stung, Susan leaned against the stone face of the

stationer's next door, clutching the aromatic, paper-wrapped loaf to her chest, the oolite Mr. Stone had found so intriguing warm and golden at her back.

The women laughed at her expense. They laughed harder when Miss Burdock said callously, her voice strong enough to carry, "It's another one-day husband she's after, that's all."

His measurements taken, a half dozen changes of clothes in the making, and a parcel full of linen undergarments and fresh neckcloths bound up with string that he might ride home with it, Philip went to the livery by way of the fruit market.

The open-air rows of boxes and baskets offered up the heavenly scent of the garden and orchard. A wealth of the local plums were in season, strawberries and raspberries as well. Gooseberries and currants soon to come, he was told. A few hothouse melons, oranges, lemons and pineapples were available, had one the currency.

Avoiding the oranges, he bought a variety of goods, all carefully packed up for him in straw wadding and nettles into two great baskets he intended to hang either side of Standard's saddle, if the animal did not object.

One of the rosy-cheeked plums he took for himself, biting into it with relish, pleased that he had accomplished so much before noon.

"Did you take Mrs. Stott's honey house then, Mr. Stone?" a familiar voice asked from behind him.

"Mr. Burdock!" He turned to face the tapman with a careful smile. "Care for a plum?"

"Don't mind if I do."

Philip began to suspect he disliked Mr. Burdock, whose strongly jowled features were not so much jovial as a studied arrangement of good cheer. The man flashed too ready a smile, too hearty his voice, his hands too swift to slap one on the back or clap a

shoulder. An ingenuine comaraderie. They were not the
good friends Mr. Burdock's tone and manner would pro-
claim them to be. Nor were they ever likely to be.

Ready to test that glib smile, the easy manner,
Philip said, "I have yet to meet your Mrs. Stott, Mr.
Burdock. It is Miss Fairford from whom I have leased
Fairford Manor."

"That's her." Burdock, nodding, took up the offered
plum with a show of yellowed teeth. "Mrs. Stott, Miss
Fairford—they are one and the same." He leaned in
close, breath smelling of onions and the local brew,
woolly brows waggling. "Though you will not hear the
young lady refer to herself by her married name."

"Nor her home as the honey house," Philip agreed,
intentionally severe, wondering if Mr. Burdock was
sanctimonious, malicious, or a combination of the two.
"She is married?" He hated himself for asking, and
yet, of all the citizens of Chipping Campden, Mr. Burdock was the most anxious to give him some insight
into the clouded past of his curious young landlady.

Burdock beamed at him. "Was married. Two sum-
mers ago. In our own St. James's by the local vicar.
All of Campden sat witness to it." He bit into the
plum with noisy relish, speaking around the juicy
bulge in his cheek. "Kissed him, she did, and accepted
his ring with many a blushing smile. Besotted, she
was."

"She is no longer married? Nulled, was it?"

Burdock grimaced and wiped a spray of juice from
his chin with the side of his hand. "I am an old-fashioned
man, Mr. Stone. I believe in the sanctity of the marriage vow no matter what the courts may say."

Wormy fruit, Philip thought, and the gentleman before him just as rotten. He cast aside the rest of his
plum.

"Miss Fairford's past . . ."

"You mean Mrs. Stott's? I call her by no other
name."

"Whatever she would call herself, surely it is her own business, and no one else's."

"I make it my business when the girl would make a public fool of herself, setting a poor example. I've a daughter, you know—a sister yet to be married. I do not like their heads and hearts tarnished with firsthand knowledge of annulments and divorces. One cannot make a maid a maid anew, once she is debauched. She is ruined in the eyes of all who know her."

"And is a man similarly ruined whenever he abandons himself to his baser needs and desires?" What would this man think of his own recent brush with love, with marriage, if he knew?

"It's different for men, Mr. Stone. Surely you agree."

If men were the ones who might be left with child after a night's passion, would not the tables be turned? "Love makes fools of the wisest of men and women, sir," Philip could not voice the words more dismissively.

Burdock shook his head, unable to follow such a concept. It proved too much for him.

Lifting his baskets, Philip bid the man good day and set off for Campden, through the Vale of Evesham, a verdant, sun-drenched ride through knob-armed ranks of apple and pear trees, green fruit swelling on the branch. And as he rode he ate, one after another, all of the tart, scarlet strawberries from the top of his basket, wondering all the while about Miss Fairford and her fruitless, foolish marriage.

Susan set to work stripping dustcovers from the furniture, one of the local girls helping her, a distant cousin of Naomi's, whom she hoped Mr. Stone would find acceptable as a maid.

Naomi came too, and Susan tried to talk her into taking the position as Mr. Stone's housekeeper, but

Naomi was more interested in asking questions about the stranger than in working for him.

"They say he is a fine figure of a man—handsome," she suggested with a sly look.

"He is not so much handsome as . . ." Susan paused to get the words right.

Naomi made a face, expression playful. "As what, Susie, my girl?"

"There is an arrogance about him, a sense of worthiness and self-confidence one rarely finds in a man so young. He carries himself with pride. As for handsome . . ." She paused, considering the memory of his face and figure. "He is well proportioned with even features."

"Ho ho!" Naomi chortled. "What else do you know of him? Tell me all. The baker's wife would have it he spent the night here, but Mrs. Burdock contradicted her. Said he lodged at the Noel Arms, upon Mr. Burdock's recommendation."

"*I* spent the night here, not Mr. Stone," Susan said.

"Did you now?" Naomi's cunning look softened. "Missing the place, were you?"

"Yes." Susan carried a dustcover to the open window to shake it.

"And Stone? Go on, girl, I'll not leave off until you tell me everything."

"He comes from Dorset, he says, along the coast."

"Has he money?" She asked the question carefully, as if afraid Susan would take offense.

Susan frowned as she folded the cloth in her hand and reached for another dustcover. "He did not blink at what I am asking for Fairford. He wants a houseful of servants, and he has gone to Evesham to fetch payment for both. Other than that, I know as much as you about our mysterious tenant."

"Do you think he could be another Mr. Stott? What do you know of this gentleman, after all? He rides into town on a good horse, well enough, but nothing else, not so much as a saddlebag the clerk at the Noel Arms tells me."

Susan lost her hold on the corner of the cloth, sending high a cloud of dust. She closed her eyes tightly, and yet it stung. Grabbing up the cloth again, she said, "There cannot be another like Stott, can there?"

Naomi leaned out of the window, shaking the cloth in her hand with such vigor it made a snapping noise. "God help Mr. Stone if he is, for I shall make mincemeat of him, my dear, before I allow another such vile creature take advantage of you."

Chapter Five

He returned to find the house unveiled, rooms overrun by strangers, dusting, polishing and washing windows. He asked if Miss Fairford was about. A girl directed him up the stairs.

She was not as easy to find as he might have imagined, her eye-catching hair doused by the pale cover of a dusting turban. He spotted her at last, leaning out of the window of the bedchamber he had in mind to make his own, vigorously shaking dustcovers, the dust catching in the breeze, whirling in a pretty, sunlit cloud about her shoulders. He leaned against the doorway to watch, intrigued by the pull of her dress across her hips. Had those hips known a man's caresses? Her husband's? Did it matter?

The older woman busy making up the bed with fresh linens peered at him around the bed curtains and cleared her throat.

"Mr. Stone, is it, sir?"

Miss Fairford turned from the window, catching her breath at sight of him, nerveless fingers letting go the dustcover. It drifted out of the window like a billowing flag.

"Oh, dear, Mr. Stone! You startled me," she said. "I'd no idea you had returned."

He held out a purse full of coins, jingling them musically. "A month's rent, Miss Fairford, as agreed upon."

She stepped away from the window to take the purse. "Thank you."

"You do not mean to count it?" His words were a challenge. He would wipe away some of her contempt with a show of gold. He was sure of it. Lavinia's eyes had always lit up at the sight.

Miss Fairfield's lips parted.

He shook his head. "You were about to say you trust me, madam, but I am a stranger to you. I insist you count it, here, before a witness."

The older woman tilted her head to gaze at him with new interest.

"I beg your pardon," Miss Fairford said. "Mr. Stone, I would introduce to you Naomi Sands. You met her boys last night."

He sketched a bow, meeting the woman's eyes, stare for stare. "And fine gentlemanly lads they are, Mrs. Sands. You are to be commended."

Miss Fairford said, "Naomi was my nanny."

"And now you labor to make me both comfortable and welcome, Mrs. Sands. Is there any possibility I might convince you to serve me in a more permanent manner while I am here in Campden?"

The older woman pursed her lips.

"I am too old, sir, with too many responsibilities of my own, to serve a man who is a mystery. I did it once. Ne'er again, for he was a rascal." She sighed, eyes fixing briefly on Miss Fairford before she plucked up a stack of dustcovers. "A houseful of servants wait to see if you will not hire them, Mr. Stone. You'll not be needin' the likes o' me. I'll just nip down and catch up the cloth you dropped, my dear." And in her every move and gesture as she made an exit, he read her complete and utter disapproval of him.

Miss Fairford moved about the room, unhurried, tucking the gold, silver and black velvet bed curtains more neatly into place, smoothing the elegant counterpane. The great four-poster bed filled the space between them all too suggestively as she did so, though she seemed unaware of its implication until she looked up, her gaze meeting his.

Had she known the pleasures of the marriage bed? Did she miss them?

She blushed, then stepped away from the bed and said, "If you will come with me," and crossed the hall to the withdrawing room, its walls lined in faded Flemish tapestries depicting the return of Ulysses to an industrious Penelope.

He thought of the missing Mr. Stott, and wondered if the industrious Miss Fairford in any way desired his return.

She sat at a delicate satinwood secretary, sunlight from the window pouring over her shoulder, tendrils of hair peeping from the turban like burnished copper thread, and he wondered what sort of man would abandon such industrious beauty. Did other men wonder, even now, how he could have abandoned Lavinia?

Pulling his coin purse from her pocket, Miss Fairford upended it without any outward show that she was impressed by the flash of his gold and began to count, neatly stacking the coins.

He held silent as she did so, fascinated all over again by the idea that she had once lived in these rooms—loved in them—that she chose now to live, instead, in a simple cottage—alone.

She took paper from the secretary—her secretary—and piling the counted coins in the middle, folded the paper into a packet around them and tucked it into her pocket. Turning, she held out to him the leather purse, on it stitched his initials—P R C, Philip Randall Chalmondeley, the R biggest, and raised, that it might stand for Rockforth as well. No S for Stone.

She cast upon him a discerning and suspicious look, brows rising.

Feeling foolish in his carelessness, he took it from her.

"What is your name, sir? Not Stone, I think."

"Perhaps not, and yet I would have the world think it is at present."

"Ah!" She rose abruptly. "Well then, Mr. Stone, I will leave you now, to better acquaint yourself with the house, and those who are eager to serve you in it."

Not she. She was not eager to serve him, to better acquaint herself with him. A shame, that.

"Does it bother you, Miss Fairford?" He stopped her in the doorway. "To know so little of my history?"

"And what I do know is clearly a lie." She met his gaze with the now familiar hint of contempt and disillusionment, as if he did but confirm her lowly expectations of men in general. "Your history is your own, whomsoever you may be, as much as mine is mine, and none of my business, or yours, unless we wish to make it otherwise."

She surprised him, the words with which she responded so like his own to Mr. Burdock that he felt them bonded in a way completely unexpected.

She seemed to think their discussion at an end. She quit the doorway for the gallery that led to the stairs.

"And do you wish it otherwise?" he asked her, following—drawn to her.

She paused, as she had the night before, on the landing, her hand curled about the newel post, the lamb on this floor, above them the shepherd and his dog, below them at the foot of the steps, crouched and waiting near the doorway, a fox. She blinked, as lost as the lamb, uncertainty in her blue eyes, as if she had yet to determine which he represented, dog or fox. "You confuse me, sir. What is it you ask of me?"

"I would know you better," he said simply.

The words hung between them in the stairwell, echoing faintly. She would not meet his gaze, her eyes fixed on the lamb. "Would you know me, or *of* me?" she murmured.

"Are they not one and the same?" he asked.

"One represents the present, the other the past."

"Which do you prefer?" he asked.

"Like you," she said, "I prefer my privacy. Is that not why you came? Why you hide your true identity?"

"You know me all too well," he said.

"I know you not at all!" She flung the contradiction at him. "And given my history, perhaps it is best kept that way."

As though that was all that needed to be said, she set off down the stairs, head high.

"Wait! Miss Fairford." He followed her. "You have gone to a great deal of trouble on short notice to clean the place, to arrange a staff for me."

"It is nothing." She lifted the dusting turban from her brow, the fiery crown of braided hair revealed.

"I do thank you, Miss Fairford. You, of all people in Campden, are entitled to the truth."

She paused on the landing to look at him, the ghostlike echo of her ancestors peering over her shoulders.

"No need," she said coolly. She rattled the paper packet of coins in her pocket. "You have paid me well enough for the privilege of anonymity."

She seemed intent on nothing but the door below them then, and leaving. He, however, was reluctant they should part, for he found her very absence of curiosity, a curiosity. Her contempt of him was a puzzle, too.

Lavinia's behavior had spawned the question. Was he, without his title, without his holdings and inheritance in some way unworthy of a woman's respect? Even a fallen woman's?

"I wonder if you would consent to taking tea with me tomorrow, after I am a little settled?"

His question stopped her in the doorway. She

turned, her fiery head already shaking in the negative, her lips parted to form the word no.

"I am sure to have questions about the house."

She pursed her lips, tucked away a straying strand of hair and nodded with a sigh. "As you wish, Mr. Stone."

He leaned against the newel post, his hand on the carved fox, her reluctance a fresh challenge. "Philip. My given name is Philip."

"Which is more inappropriate, Mr. Stone? Referring to you by the name I know to be a lie, or by your given name, when I haven't the least idea who you really are?"

He had no answer to that. Nor did she seem to expect one.

A ghostly apparition drifted through the garden at noon the following day, faceless and white. He caught sight of it through the window as he stepped dripping from the polished wood bathtub. His temporary valet, Perry, a sparse old gent, held linen ready for him. He wrapped his torso and draped his shoulders in another length, the linen stiff with newness. Twined S's along the borders. He examined them with interest, running his finger along the blue thread, wondering if Stott was buried beneath the rose bushes, his ghost wandering the garden in the middle of the day.

"Susan Stott she was to have been," the old man said. He nodded at the window, as if he, too, saw the phantom. "Embroidered them herself, she did. Hadn't the heart to rip them up. I found them at the back of the linen press. I hope you do not mind using them, sir. I thought, given your name is Stone . . ."

Philip nodded with a wry laugh, fingering the S's again, thinking of the stitchery of his leather coin purse. He could not tell the man the name Stone suited him no better than Stott suited Miss Fairford.

He took the linen from his shoulders with a rueful

grin to rub at his hair, moving closer to the window, that he might examine better the ghost in the garden, not ghost at all, but Miss Fairford, fiery hair hidden in a pale hat, her face and shoulders draped in pale leno. White gloves guarded her hands. She drifted languidly through the hives, sliding something that glinted in the sun like great knives meant to layer straw cakes into the lower half of each of the beehives.

"She employed you when Stott disappointed her?"

"Yes, sir. I served Mr. Fairford as valet before he died, and Miss Fairford as butler when she came into the inheritance he left her."

"She is well provided for, then?"

"She was, until Stott came along. He stole more than her heart, you see."

Philip thought of Lavinia as he ran a comb through his hair, and held out his arms for one of the shirts he had purchased in Evesham. Was it only his wealth she had wanted when she had stolen his heart? And he unwilling to see it?

He stepped into his stockings and britches, then paused by the window to watch Miss Fairford, with whom he had far more in common than she realized.

"Is it safe? What she is doing?" he asked.

She had lifted from the top of the hives, one by one, the straw domes, and beneath them, with small square plates, carefully adjusted something golden that glinted in the sunlight.

"The bees, sir? It's never them that stung her, sir."

Slowly, the world moved slowly, constantly on the edge of danger, when Susan walked among the hives. Behind the mistlike cover of her white leno veil, pulse slightly accelerated, sweat gathering on her brow, the world, past and future, was cut off. There was only now the harsh sound of her own breathing, the pounding of her heart, and the ceaseless buzzing of the bees.

She turned slowly, everything must be done slowly

around bees, to find Mr. Stone, or whomever he might really be with the initials PRC, stopped beside the garden path, watching her intently. Why had he come to Chipping Campden, this man who lied about his identity, just as Stott had? Why did she pull in liars, she wondered, like bees to honey?

"Far enough, Mr. Stone," she said low-voiced, the delivery of her words as steady as the course of her hands to the covered basket into which she placed the lidded honey jar. "I would advise you not to come closer."

She turned to replace the full bell-shaped jar with an identical empty one, her movements controlled despite the nervousness this man aroused.

The taking of the honey often drew observers. Her father's friends, the servants, had always been fascinated. Mr. Stott, too, had claimed interest and fear that she would be stung, when it was he she ought to have been warned against.

Her mysterious tenant had sense enough not to distract her with questions when she stood too close to the hive.

"Have you never been stung?" he asked when she stepped away again, the second jar in hand. Awe colored his voice—a sweet sound.

She capped the honey and crossed to where he stood beside her basket.

"When I am stupid to their ways," she admitted, tucking the jar into her basket and taking up a clean one. Her eyes met his. "But I have learned to step lightly among creatures who might hurt me."

She returned to the hive, carefully positioned the fresh jar and covered it with the woven straw dome.

"You look different today, Mr. Stone."

"Oh?"

"Your hair. Is it darker than usual?"

He raised his hand self-consciously to his head. "It

is wet, Miss Fairford. I have been trying out your bath."

Had he bathed in honor of her coming to tea? The idea alarmed her a little. She realized she feared him in exactly the same way she had always feared the bees, the way she should have feared Mr. Stott—a fear of latent danger, of potential harm. Or was it passion she really feared? Would her own affections sting her again?

She stilled such thoughts and reminded herself to move slowly in taking another jar from its hive.

"You seem completely fearless among them," he said, voice low, as she approached. "At home among bees."

She smiled, free to smile beneath the veil, hidden. "I always imagined myself a sort of bee bride when I tended the hives as a girl, veiled in white, my movements slow, graceful, deliberate."

"Ah!" The upward curve of his lips transformed his face.

Susan thought of how she had described him to Naomi when she had asked if he was a handsome man. She had refrained from saying he was when he smiled. His lips, indeed, had always seemed handsome to her—provocative.

She thought of Stott, always smiling, the worker bee—busy with paperwork, buzzing with purpose and honeyed promises that had never materialized—a business, a bank account, a town house in London. Lies, all lies. The greatest lie of all the name he would give her. There was no Theodore Stott.

She shoved home the last zinc plate beneath glowing golden jar, carefully lifted it, capped it and turned to her basket, to the man who lied about his name as much as Stott had.

"Bees are easy," she said calmly. "Far easier than people."

"How so?" He stepped forward to open the basket, anticipating her need.

She held high the jar, admiring the glistening comb within. "Bees are so very clear in their purpose—in their reason for existing. Queens, drones, workers, each diligent in their own industry: propagation of the species, the gathering of flower nectar and the care of the hive."

She turned the jar. "I love the orderly elegance of their combs, am ever amazed by their abundant production—unending golden riches. People"—she sighed, thinking of Stott, of the mystery of the initials PRC—"are far more complicated. Would you not agree?"

"Have we not in society our own workers and drones, our own queens and kings?" He seemed in a mood to debate the matter.

"In a way." She took up the last empty jar. "But there are no liar bees, are there? No robber bees to steal honey from one another. It is the beekeeper who is thief."

"And provider," he reminded her. "For did you not give these bees homes, and a garden of many blossoms from which to gather nectar?"

She smiled beneath her veil, bee bride that she was, and nodded at his wisdom, then turning, went to set in place the empty jar, that she might rob from her well-tended bee subjects again in future.

Philip thought of his brother as the fearless Miss Fairford replaced the last straw dome and gently withdrew the zinc plates that had separated her from harm. Brett had experimented with hives when they were boys.

But this pretty hooded creature was not the ghost of his childhood. Carrying the zinc plates to where he stood, Miss Fairford accepted his offer of assistance in helping her transport everything to the buttery for a wash.

There, honey-stained gloves removed, she lifted the hat and veil from her fiery locks. Sweat dewed her brow and upper lip. Her complexion was flushed like a woman's in love.

He remembered Lavinia's face the morning he had left her, similarly flushed.

He said without thinking, "You will be wanting to use your bath again."

Miss Fairford gazed at him a moment in wide-eyed, breathless silence.

"No? A basin and pitcher, then? Something to cool your brow? Whatever you deem appropriate. Simply ask one of the maids. I shall be in the red withdrawing room, drafting a letter to my solicitor. Perhaps you will join me there when you are more comfortable?"

Chapter Six

"Let me help with that, Betty," Susan offered.

"No, no, miss." The older woman clutched tighter the basin, linen, soap and steaming pitcher she carried into what had once been Susan's room. "Let me pretend it is the old days for a moment. I miss them, marm. I miss you."

Susan stopped on the threshold, feeling completely out of place. "Mr. Stone does not use this room?"

"Oh, no, miss. Said, seeing as it was yours he could not see fit to intrude upon it. He has taken the guest chamber to sleep in."

"Has he?"

"Yes, marm. He did make a point of asking which room had been your father's, and though he liked the view, and commented favorably on the bedstead and tapestries, in the end he decided against it."

Susan wondered it he did so arbitrarily, or out of consideration for her feelings. Whatever the reason, it pleased her that he chose to avoid intruding upon bedchambers so charged with memory and meaning to her.

Betty settled her burden on the washstand in the corner and tipped the cheval mirror for a better view.

Susan took one rueful look at her overheated face and understood why her mystery tenant had suggested she might like a bath. Red blotches uglied her cheeks and neck, beads of sweat gathered beneath her lower lip and trickled from her temples.

"Oh, my," she said. "Only look at me. I am supposed to take tea with Mr. Stone this afternoon."

"And so you shall, miss. Turn around. We've only to unlace you, pass a sponge and a bit of soap over all, and you will feel fresh as ever."

Susan obeyed, stepping from her dress, standing arms held wide and to the sides as she submitted to a sponge bath, clad only in her undergarments. Susan took comfort in Betty's unruffled calm. Her gaze met the maid's in the mirror.

"Ah, Betty, how do I manage without you?"

Betty's eyes gleamed with a sudden welling of unshed tears. She swiftly blinked them away and gave Susan's hand a comforting pat. "Quite well, it would seem, marm. There were many as said you would not manage without a husband or wait staff in your reduced circumstances, but I knew better. Told 'em you could and would. And look at you now, leasing the house—making do nicely in your town cottage, trading your honey."

"I had hoped to lure a tenant who wished to take the house for much longer. I worry that just such an opportunity may be missed in leasing the place for such a short time to Mr. Stone."

"You worry too much," Betty scolded.

"Mmmm, that feels much cooler." Susan managed a weak smile as she sank back upon her beloved bed, clad only in her chemise. The feather mattress clutched at her, reminding her of the years she had indulged herself in the luxury of its comfort without true appreciation for what she had.

"Oh, Betty!" She flung her arm across her brow, guarding her eyes from view of embroidered bed hangings and ornate, plaster-daddoed ceiling, everywhere reminders of all that she had lost to her own foolishness. "I am myself unconvinced I can survive on my own."

"Nah, nah, now, miss. I'll not hear such talk." The

clink of a glass stopper and the familiar odor of vinegar filled the room. "Come. A few minutes without the sun beating upon your head, and a cool vinegar compress upon your temples, and we shall banish such unworthy thoughts. You're a brave lass, you are, to go it alone. I know that your father's friend, Sir Gregory Wraxall, offered to marry you, and that you declined his offer kindly."

"However did your hear that?" Susan pulled the compress from her forehead and sat up again. "I have not told a soul."

"Tut, tut. Wraxall's Minnie is a friend of mine. She knew when he took you for a stroll with the dogs to see the new lambs what it was he meant to say to you."

"A kind man," Susan said, remembering that day, wondering ever so briefly if she had been a fool to turn down the security Wraxall had offered. "A dear old man."

Betty winked at her. "Too old, my dear. Minnie agreed with me. She even said Sir Gregory looked rather relieved when you had gone away."

Susan laughed. "He told me he had a fondness for me, but I knew he felt it his duty to help me out of loyalty to Father."

"Shall we take down your hair, miss? And dress it afresh?"

"Please do. Will you do it in fine looping plaits the way you used to? I cannot tell you how many times I have tried to duplicate the style without success."

"Happy to, miss. I shall go slow, shall I? With the mirror, just so? There. You can see how it is done."

He sat at the desk by the window trying to compose a letter to Pritney, Watts, and Dover, his solicitors, trying not to think about Miss Fairford in the room next door, trying not to overhear the woman's voices drifting in on the breeze.

And yet, as wrong as it was to eavesdrop, he did not stop. He pretended to resharpen a quill with a pretty little silver knife from the desk, while with every passing minute his interest was sharpened in Miss Susan Fairford, their misfortunes a link he had never expected to find here in the Cotswolds.

The house he temporarily called his own, the servants who saw so diligently to his comfort had once been hers. She had been offered a comfortable marriage and had refused it on principle. He could not help but think of Lavinia. What had he found to so admire in her? To blind him to her devices? She had accepted his offer of marriage, out of what—pure greed? Did she care for him at all? Had he any true evidence of it?

"What do you think of him?" Betty was saying.

Him, who? he wondered, the knife slipping from his hand and bouncing away beneath the secretary. He pushed back his chair and bent to pick it up.

"I do not know him well enough to offer an opinion," Susan said.

Did they mean him? His head came up in a hurry. Too much of a hurry, he rapped his skull against the edge of the bottom drawer of the secretary. Like a jack-in-the-box, out popped the drawer.

"He has the bearing and appearance of the well-to-do," Betty said. "But he brings nothing with him but a horse. Running from trouble, do you think?"

Philip rubbed his bruised pate as he considered the trouble he ran from. Not at all the sort they might suppose.

"I would not care to speculate," Miss Fairford said, and he liked her the more for her unwillingness.

"Not even after Stott?" Betty asked.

"Especially after Mr. Theodore Stott. I made the mistake of guessing, of assuming, far too much where he was concerned. I refuse to make the same mistake again."

"Do you never call him Ted anymore then, miss? You did once utter his given name as if it were precious to you."

"I was young then—naive and trusting. I'll not easily lose my heart again."

Distracted, thinking of how a woman sounded in uttering a name as if it were precious to her, Philip carelessly tipped the inkstand and came close to knocking it off the desk entirely, but in the last instant righted it. A blot spattered the sheet of foolscap on which he had been scribbling. He folded the paper, creating a larger inkblot, obliterating most of what he had written.

The letter was unimportant. Would that the pages of one's life might so easily be rewritten. He remembered clearly now. Lavinia had uttered a name as if it were precious to her on their wedding day.

It had not been his.

Susan found him standing at the withdrawing room window, quill in hand, ink staining the pointer finger of his right hand, his eyes on the garden, the fingers of his left gently stroking the feather. A dove cried mournfully from the treetops, a warbler babbled in the shrubbery, a thrush sang *seep-seep* from the peak of the roof. She wondered if he heard them, if he appreciated the beauty of the view, of the house. She wondered who it was he wrote to. Creditors? Money lenders? A sweetheart he abandoned?

"Come in, Miss Fairford. Come in," he suggested when she paused in the doorway.

"Have you eyes in the back of your head, Mr. Stone?" she asked.

"No. The windowpane held your reflection."

He turned to face her, a smile on his lips. Those lips, that smile, unsettled the rhythm of her heart every time he allowed it freedom—no matter how much she steeled herself against it.

"Do I interrupt your letter?" she asked uneasily.

He waved at a blotched page. "It will not word itself, and I have spilled ink over what little I managed. No matter. I will make another attempt before the sun sets."

He put down the quill, noticing the stain on his hand with a frown.

She went swiftly to the secretary, where she took from the bottom drawer a stained rag and a bottle she kept for just such purpose.

His brow cleared when she handed it to him. "How thoughtful you are." He unstoppered the bottle, releasing the strong smell of spirits as he wet the rag. "Would that we might as easily remove all life's blots."

He rubbed at the ink.

"How else may I help you?" she asked.

He looked up, eyes bright, brows arching, as if her remark surprised him. "Am I in need of assistance?"

"You wished to know more about the house?"

He stoppered the bottle, his gaze less distant than in the past. "I wonder that you can bear to watch another claim it, even briefly."

She avoided his gaze, eyes misting. "A house should be lived in." She felt the need to straighten a mountain landscape, to adjust the position of the needlepoint firescreen, to wind the ormulu clock upon the mantel.

He stood quiet, watching.

"The servants? They are to your liking?"

"All save that of housekeeper."

"Naomi offends you?"

"Naomi would not agree to fill the post." He ruefully stoppered the bottle. "She claims she is too old to work for a young liar."

Susan laughed, quickly stifling the sound, for in laughter she let her guard down and lost all wariness of him. She could not allow herself to too quickly trust in him, no matter how likeable he might be.

"Naomi is not one to couch her opinions," she said.

He nodded and stepped to the secretary, the light from the window turning his hair the color of bullion. She felt sure he intended to put away the rag and spirits bottle, and while it pleased her that he wished to keep the room tidy, she knew he would have trouble with the drawer. It had a secret catch at the base.

She went to help, bending beside him, close enough that the skirt of his coat brushed the skirt of her gown.

"There is—" she said.

"A catch, I know." Voice low, his fingers closed over hers, the mechanism sinking beneath their combined pressure, his hand warm and firm against hers.

Her head turned, so close, his breath burned against her cheek. She froze, heart running like a rabbit, all stops and starts and erratic changes in direction.

"Beg pardon," he said.

They both backed away as if bitten, stealing uncomfortable looks at one another. The tension she experienced in his company increased tenfold.

The entire exchange lasted but an instant.

The skin of her hand, her cheek, seemed forever changed. She wondered for a brief, heated moment what it would be like to lose her way with such a man, as she had lost her way with Stott. Theodore Stott's lips, though warm, had never fired her skin to such a heated sensitivity—his breath on her cheek had never left her knees boneless as pudding.

In that instant Susan Fairford feared Mr. Philip Stone, whoever he might be, with all of her heart and soul. If Stott could so easily kiss away her common sense, what might this man do?

"I found your secret catch quite by accident. I hope you do not mind." His voice was level, his gaze steady, as if their recent physical contact left him unmoved.

He calmly slid open her secret drawer as if it were his own. "I wonder if I might convince you to do it?"

"It?" The word seemed a complete non sequitur, dangerous in its very lack of specificity.

He turned, his eyes very green, all their focus on her, his stance still far closer than she cared for—the potential of "it" daunting.

"Would you consider serving me . . ."

He dampened his lips with the tip of his tongue, as if to ask her made him uneasy. She thought again of kisses, of the ways a woman might serve a man.

He sighed, his lips moving, those damnably captivating lips. "I can think of no one who knows the place or servants so well. They would clearly take their orders from you without quibbling."

She blinked, undone by her own hubris. He wished her to serve as housekeeper!

"Oh. No! I cannot," she blurted instinctively. She could not lower herself. To accept would stir gossip. It would place her too intimately in this stranger's company.

"Playing housekeeper in your own house. Do I ask too much? It need not occupy your whole day."

"Really, I . . ."

He seemed prepared for her objection. "It is only two weeks, perhaps three."

"I do not think . . ."

"Simply drop by and see things are set right of a morning, and pop in of an afternoon to see if anything untoward has developed—if questions require answering, or squabbles resolving."

"Mr. Stone . . ."

"I would pay you well," he promised, his lips firm in making the promise.

Tempting. She heard echo in her mind of Mr. Stott, smelling of cheroot, leaning over her shoulder, whispering in her ear, *I will treat you well.*

She shook her head, troubled by the idea of refusing desperately needed money. "I shall give it thought."

"Excellent. Perhaps we can sort it out over tea in the garden." He rose from the chair at the secretary, and with a bow indicated she should precede him down the stairs.

As they made their way, he said, "One other thing I would beg you to consider, Miss Fairford."

She moved swiftly, the steps familiar. She was eager to be free of the house, of his requests. "Yes?"

Into the sunshine they stepped, and still he had not answered. The smell of bruised marjoram sweetened their passage as he opened the gate for her into the garden.

"I have word that there is a vehicle such as I am in need of hiring, in a nearby village called Long . . ."

"Compton?" She bent to pluck a bracket of leaves, winding it about her fingers, the scent as strong as her suspicion he knew already she intended a trip tomorrow to Long Compton.

"I wondered . . ." He paused uneasily.

"You know of my honey run?"

"Would you mind me accompanying you?"

She fingered the aromatic leaves uneasily. She had not ridden the lanes in the company of a gentleman since Stott.

"Betty mentioned you were going my direction. I would not intrude if it is inconvenient, or if you care not for company—"

"No, no," she stopped him, feeling foolish in her very reluctance. "Of course I am happy to show you the way. It is only . . . that your progress needs be slow in my company. I make several stops that will delay you. You would likely get there much faster by way of the main road, though it is the longer way."

A table and chairs had been set up in the rose garden, as he had asked, a teapot, butter, strawberry pre-

serves and fresh scones issued from the kitchen as they
took their seats.

He made sure she took the chair facing away from
the sun, her hair become thus a glowing nimbus, the
sky bent on rivaling the celestial blue of her eyes,
the strawberries less tempting lure than the fruit of
her lips.

"About your honey run . . ."

He wondered what she thought of him as their eyes
met. Could she, he wondered, could any woman ever
care for him as he had wanted Lavinia to? What had
Miss Fairford done to make a husband run away from
her—as he had fled Lavinia?

Her lips parted on her reply.

He held up his hand to stay her.

"I've a selfish reason for wishing to accompany
you."

"Oh?"

"Yes. I understand that you hire the local hack that
I had hoped to take with me in case Standard has no
taste for traces. He is a saddle horse. I have never
attempted to put him to a carriage. Rather than allow
him to kick the gig in question into firewood I
thought . . ."

"You are welcome to the hack. I shall simply go
another day."

He made a discontented noise in his throat. "That
does not suit me. It makes perfect sense to me that
we should kill two birds with one stone. You ride the
hack, introduce me to a few of the locals, show me
the way, and I shall offer you a ride home in the gig."

"I see. It would seem you have this thing well
thought out." She eyed him over the rim of her cup
with the suspicion he grew used to seeing in her eyes.

"Convinced?" he asked.

"There are no inns or posting houses along the
lanes I take," she warned.

He grasped at once the drawback. "Shall I have Cook pack refreshments?"

She nodded with some reluctance, her glance when it fell on him always wary, as if she knew better than to trust him.

"Kidney pies," she said. "If she will make them."

Susan went at once upon the conclusion of their tea to fetch from Mr. Jenks, the hostler at the Red Lion, the hack she always hired to take her on her honey runs.

"A bit earlier than usual to fetch the beast," Jenks remarked.

"Yes. I've a mind to ride him this afternoon, to Evesham."

"Business at the market, have you, miss?" he asked.

"Business, yes," she replied evasively.

"I shall expect him back again by sundown tomorrow, then?"

"Without fail," she agreed as he helped her into the saddle.

Within the hour she rode into Evesham, making her way at once, not to the market, but to the bank, where she closeted herself away with none other than Mr. Buttersby, who rose from his chair to greet her with officious fervor.

"Come in, come in, Miss Fairford. How can I help you? I understand you have a new tenant at Fairford."

"Yes. I have come to you regarding said tenant, Mr. Stone," she said, "whose business I recommended your way."

Buttersby steepled his fingers and raised his brows, as if surprised. "I am much obliged Miss Fairford, but how can I help you, that Mr. Stone might not better?"

"I know, as you must also know, the name Stone to be false. Having once been fooled by a man bearing a false name, I would know who my tenant is. And as he does not tell me, I thought perhaps you might be so good.''

Buttersby cleared his throat, as if her request were unpleasantly stuck there. "All of my clients' business is strictly confidential, Miss Fairford. Surely that comes as no surprise to you."

Susan folded her hands in her lap and with bowed head said, "You must tell me, Mr. Buttersby. You owe it to me."

Buttersby's steepled fingers fell to clutching at one another atop the much used blotter protecting his desktop. "I cannot, Miss Fairford. You know I cannot. It would be entirely unethical for me to breathe a word, especially as his lor . . . er . . . Mr. Stone, made explicit point of swearing me to silence."

She caught the slip of his tongue, thought she knew what he had been about to say, but carefully gave no sign of it. Instead, she lifted her chin, took a deep breath and forced herself to confront him. "You speak to me of ethics, Mr. Buttersby. Was it ethical of you to breathe no word to me of Mr. Stott's financial state before our marriage? To see so swiftly, so efficiently to a transfer of funds the instant I was wed? You helped Stott to rob me blind, sir. Who, I ask you, was left to pay the debts you so ethically kept secret?"

Buttersby blushed, his hands awkward now, playing with the quill from his ink standish, and yet he had nothing to say.

Susan tried again. "This gentleman, Mr. Stone, is my tenant. You know he is. I risk my only remaining asset, Fairford Manor, if he is not what he claims to be. If he is, in fact, another Stott."

"I gave my word, Miss Fairford." He sat forward and shook his head, eyes roving the room, a trace of perspiration dewing his forehead, his manner that of a trapped animal. "Lord knows, I would not have you remain uneasy. I am sorry for any past omissions, but let me assure you, though in some ways a mystery,

Mr. Stone is a man of some standing, a gentleman of means, not a person who has need to cheat you."

"You mean to calm me? And yet you admit he is not what or whom he claims to be!" She allowed emotion to creep into her voice, which rose a notch. A mistake. Her show of emotion lessened his. It stiffened his resolve against her immediately.

He sat back, features closed, eyes gone cold. "I admit nothing. And you show yourself ungrateful with these histrionics. They are quite uncalled for. You must trust me in this. I keep nothing from you that might bring you harm. Now, if you've no other business with me, I will bid you good day."

She went away, little wiser.

Chapter Seven

The following day dawned cool and still, the sky cloudless, a tissue of pale blue, the sun brightening the grass, the nodding faces of the wildflowers along the road deepening the cool shadow beneath the trees. There was a bright stillness to the High Street as Susan met Philip outside her door. He got down to help her load the hack with baskets of straw nested honey pots.

She took advantage of a mounting block outside her door to step into the sidesaddle. He held the hack's head while she arranged her skirt.

"An unnecessary courtesy, Mr. Stone," she said, maintaining the same wary posture that stiffened her back whenever they met. He had never seen a woman so uncomfortable in his presence. She seemed always on her guard, as if he meant her ill. Yesterday's tea had gone awkwardly. Her manner remained too formal, too distant.

She was right, of course. The horse was the most docile plug he had ever set eyes upon, but it was polite in him to hold the horse, nonetheless. It would have been polite in her to thank him.

Swinging into the saddle himself, they set out slowly, side by side, her attention fixed on the baskets behind her. She did, in fact, stop and ask him, "Please wait a minute, Mr. Stone. My pots are knocking."

He wanted to laugh. There was something inherently funny in what she had said, and yet her face

bore no trace of amusement, and so he turned Standard that he might listen for the sound as the hack
plodded past, and assisted in adjusting the straw wadding until all traveled with a minimum of jiggling.

He did not often see her smile. Had he ever heard
her laugh?

A few of the shopkeepers along the High Street
drifted into doorways to watch, nodding as they
passed, clearly curious to see them together.

"Where are you two off to, then?" the vicar did not
hesitate to ask as they passed him.

They reined in their horses.

Miss Fairford made introductions.

Philip doffed the new broad-brimmed hat he had
brought back with him from Evesham, knowing the
vicar wanted a look, to judge him fit company for one
of his parishioners.

"We are for Long Compton. I've a mind to hire a
gig." His voice carried in the still air. The whole village would know their destination before sunset.
Philip intended they should. He would rather that they
knew at once the truth rather than stew in speculation
the entire time they were gone.

"Who is it you mean to have the gig from?" the
vicar asked.

"A gentleman by the name of Foster."

"If it is David Foster you mean, you need not fear
he will cheat you," the vicar assured him.

There would be gossip anyway, a young woman riding out alone with a stranger.

"Do you care to come with us, vicar?" Philip canted
his head, squinting, to study the older gentleman's reaction, to glimpse Susan Fairford's face as well. "Miss
Fairford has been kind enough to invite me to accompany her on her honey run, as I do not know my
way." He lifted the hat, using it like a shield to block
the glare of the sun. "We've a fine day for it."

The vicar looked upon him with canny kindliness.

"I thank you for asking, sir. I am very pleased you should think to include me." His gaze drifted to Susan and back again. "Regretfully, I must decline. Much to do, you know. Do you mean to stop in at the Miller's?" he asked Susan.

She nodded.

"Will you be so good as to tell William I shall visit him before the week is out?"

"But of course," she said, a careful set to her mouth, as if this mention of the Millers meant more than he understood. She drew a breath, forced a stiff smile and said, "I mean to drop in on the Kelly's, Nell Blackman and Sir Gregory as well. Shall I send them your greetings, Vicar? Perhaps you will have time to check in with all of them."

Ah! The vicar intended to check their progress, did he?

The vicar smiled, as if pleased she understood his warning, "You must tell them I expect to see them in church this Sunday," he said pleasantly. "May I count on the two of you, Miss Fairford? Mr. Stone?"

"In every way," Philip said.

The two men shared a nod, shared an understanding, too. Miss Fairford was not to be trifled with. With a cluck of the tongue to their horses, Susan and Philip rode on.

"Did you really want the vicar to come?" she asked when they had turned the corner at the end of the street.

"I wanted him to feel there was no reason he should not," Philip said.

"Ah." For the first time he could remember she looked at him with something akin to admiration.

Philip basked in it, pleased.

They guided their horses out of the town, past the rattle and hum of the silk mill, beyond the turnoff to the quarry from which the oolite was mined, away from the coach road that led to Banbury, into the narrower lane that would take them to Paxford—the peaceful ford, he remembered his Latin—as if the disturbing stillness of the day needed added peace.

He was unaccustomed to such stillness, to gently waving grasses and a faint stirring of the trees. The coast of Devon was rarely without a bit of wind. Here there was no swell of the ocean, no salt in the breeze, merely a patchwork of green as far as the eye could see—behind them the escarpment, and in the fields before them dots of white, the fat, broad-faced local sheep interrupting the quiet with occasional plaintive bleeting.

This green splendor was alien to him—pleasant, but strange. He was accustomed to wide-open spaces, merrem grass bent double in the wind, stunted elms braced against rocky cliffs and always in the background the rushing voice of the sea.

The absence of the great spread of sky and sea, of movement, always movement, in some way alarmed him, as did his own languid doldrums, his retreat from all responsibility. Here he drifted, rudderless, useless, at odds with time and purpose.

Even the steady thump of the horses' hooves along the dirt road was at odds with the clatter of hooves and wheels, his carriage rushing, always rushing to get somewhere soon, for there was much to be done, people to see, decisions to be made, engagements to fulfill, and here he had none of it.

They must go slow in order not to break the honey pots, but the languid sun-in-his-face backroad saunter felt all wrong, pent-up and breathless, almost painful, as if something unexpected must happen. It had been just such a day that he had almost wed Lavinia, just such a glorious, sun-drenched day he had ridden hell-for-leather through the country that had taken him away from her.

Miss Fairford seemed to relish the stillness, the sweet, grassy morning air, the cloudless swatches of sky. She looked about her bright-eyed and joyful, breathing deep, smiling squint-eyed into the sun, curls like polished brass against her cheek. He wondered if she thought of the mysterious Mr. Stott in quiet moments like this.

"A glorious morning," she said, inhaling deeply, and for the first time since they had met, she smiled.

They stopped at four places along their way, two between Paxford and Todham, one on the way to Great Wolford, the last on the far side of Barton-on-Heath. Beans, turnips, barley and tasseled corn they saw aplenty, red poppies and corncockle sprouting between the rows. Cotswold and Leicester sheep sprinkled whitely across green pastures, cattle, too, Herefords and Gloucesters and oxen bred from the two.

"Friends of my father," she said after the first couple, the Kellys, kept them chattering for a good three-quarters of an hour, and plied them with fresh-baked bread and a wee nip of cider.

He was introduced as "the new tenant of Fairford Hall," said title earning him a great deal of delving curiosity and kindly urgings to help himself to more cider, more bread and butter. Did he care for a pup? One of their collie bitches had just delivered a litter.

He politely refused. "I've four dogs at home: Jacko, Trouble, Button and Pierce."

Susan—no one along their journey called her anything so formal as Miss Fairford—evidenced surprise at this mention of pets. "What sort of dogs are they?"

"Mastiff, Newfoundland, a King Charles spaniel and a fox terrier."

This information would seem to please her, as if the ownership of dogs in some way made him a better man.

Talk centered first on sheepherding dogs, then sheep—how the weather affected the herd of late, the condition of the turnip and hay crop that must feed the sheep through winter, how well the lambing had gone, and the new breeds that were being crossed with the Cotswold and Leicestershire.

Maggots, too, must be discussed, the shepherd's wet weather bane. Miss Fairford held forth intelligently on all levels of discussion while Philip fell quiet and listened. Of all his many investments, land improvements, shipping ventures and possessions, sheep was not one of them.

"They are good folk," Susan said as they rode away. He began to think of her as Susan that day.

"The best," he said. "They managed to make me feel both welcome and on guard."

"On guard?"

"Yes. They hold you precious, and let me know of it in no uncertain terms."

"They have been good to me, since . . ."

"Since your father died?"

"Well . . . yes," she faltered uncertainly.

"Do you mind my asking—did he make his fortune in wool trading?"

"He did. Why?"

"The staircase at Fairford."

"Of course. The newel posts."

"Poor lamb," he said. "Trapped forever between the fox and the dog, and likely to be eaten in the end by either."

She laughed. "Since I was a little girl, my favorite of the carvings has been the dog. Faithful creature. I just knew he went to battle with the fox in the middle of the night when no one was looking, in order to save that poor carved lamb."

"And the faces in the Great Hall? Were you convinced they turned head to follow your passage about the room at night?"

She smiled. He liked to see her smile, the sun full upon her face, the blue of her eyes as cloudless as the sky.

"Your imagination runs away with you, Mr. Stone."

"I ran away, right enough. But it took very little imagination," he said ruefully.

She gave him a searching look. He guarded his expression, unwilling to tell her more, unwilling to remember again why he had run.

They rode on in silence until they reached the second of the farms to which she delivered, this one grander than the first, the buildings ancient, timbered, the rooftops thickly thatched. Medieval, he guessed, well kept. A pack of happy, yelping sheep dogs and three gamboling children ran out to greet them—to greet her—it seemed she was a favorite with the Millers.

He enjoyed this chance to see Susan Fairford among others, gently ordering the dogs to sit, scratching with fond expression their ears, while she asked the children had they been berry picking lately, and how did they do in the learning of their letters, and what had the youngest done to earn such a vivid grass stain upon his knee?

The Millers were fine, unprepossessing folk, dressed with a mind to the practical rather than fashionable, their arms open to welcome Miss Fairford and her honey pots, with cries of "How do you do?" and "Come in. Come in. Who is this gentleman you bring with you?"

Mr. Stone was met with wary politeness, searching looks and the same questions that had buzzed about him during the first of her deliveries. What part of the country did he hale from? What business brought him to Chipping Campden? How long did he intend to stay?"

He kept his answers brief, the lies to a minimum. He began to hate the very idea of Mr. Stone from the coast of Dorset, relaxing for a fortnight in the countryside, spreading lies for the Marquess of Chalmondeley, Earl of Rockforth.

Miss Fairford seemed not to notice the brevity of his responses, the rote repetition of his explanations. Her manner was relaxed and warm, her honey pots paid for not in coin but in trade. They took away with them fresh loaves of bread, a wheel of cheese, potted meats, eel and goose liver, butter and mustard. She was offered a leg of lamb, and begged that she might be allowed to pick it up upon their return that afternoon, for then they might have the gig in which to transport it.

They were on their way again, just the two of them, a trifle less awkward than before, side by side in the quiet loneliness of the lane, the sun higher, brighter, the cool moist smell of the morning's dew burned away, the birds less vocal, marjoram, sainfoin and the blue meadow cranesbill nodding at them from the lane's verges. Winchats, stonechats, pippits, corn buntings, whitethroats and an occasional kestral or lapwing erupted in a flurry of wings from the hedgerows before the plodding approach of the horses. Rabbits and the larger brown hares hopped away through the grass.

She loved the lanes, loved the honey run. So much verdant green and the air cool upon her cheeks, the steady, plodding gait of the horse beneath her hip, calmed her.

"It is beautiful here," he said, and it pleased her he should think so though she reminded herself it should not matter one way or the other what he thought.

"Is the countryside much different where you come from, Mr. Stone?" she asked.

"Yes. A different sort of beauty."

"Tell me. I have never been outside of Gloucestershire."

"Ah, but you must see the coast one day."

His voice held an affection she had not expected. It stirred her.

"The green, not of grass, but of placid sea."

He closed his eyes, pale lashes thick upon his cheek.

"You cannot completely understand the beauty of England"—he looked up, gesturing toward the clouds—"until you have heard the gulls, like the sky opening on rusted hinges, until you have watched the quick-footed dance of the sandpiper, in and out and in and out at water's edge."

His fingers demonstrated the dancing gait.

She sat her horse, awestruck that a man revealed his appreciation of his surroundings so poetically.

"You have not lived," he went on, "until you have stood on the windblown crest of a plunging cliffline to breathe deep the briny smell—to admire the lace of foam upon the heaving breast of a silvered sea."

The images caught at her heart and imagination. She could picture him there, hair blowing in the wind. "You sound homesick," she said.

He turned to look at her with the distant green eyes she had never imagined saw the world so vividly. She wondered how well he saw her, and in what terms he would describe her, if asked.

"I did not expect to miss it, but I do."

"Why did you leave in such a hurry, sir, if you love it so?"

He shifted in the saddle, leather creaking, leaning forward to clap his mount's neck, to stroke his mane. "Have you ever caught yourself, Miss Fairford, on the brink of a colossal misjudgment of character?"

She frowned. Was it Stott he meant?

"Ever thought you knew someone as well as one might, only to discover all that you held true to be mistaken?"

Of course. Stott. With swiftly rising ire she regarded him from beneath the pale brim of her bonnet. He saw her well enough, too well perhaps. The keenness of his question touched upon all that was yet raw and unhealed within her.

"If you know anything of my misfortunes, Mr. Stone," she said very coldly, "you cannot but be aware that I have, indeed, made just such unpleasant discoveries too late to avoid their dire consequences."

He studied her until the silence weighed heavy between them. "Consequences. Yes. I had no desire to face them. That is why I left in such a hurry. I looked upon the face of Medusa and was changed to stone."

"And has she snakes for hair, as reputed?" she asked, voice brittle, disarmed to discover he referred to his own troubles, not hers.

"Snakes?"

She expected a laugh. He merely nodded sadly and said, "Yes, a head full of snakes."

The air seemed charged with his words, with their private significance.

"And what were you before she changed you?" she asked carefully, knowing he revealed something important of himself, and yet not at all sure what it was.

"I . . ." He sighed. "I was a man in love. I wanted to marry Medusa, you see? I had not recognized her for what she was."

That he spoke of a woman, and that she had hurt him deeply was clear, all else obfuscation.

"And will you polish your shield, Mr. Stone? Make a mirror for her to look upon? Medusa's spell can thus be broken I have read."

"A mirror?" He turned the gentle green of his eyes upon her, gaze intense, delving, as if he looked for something lost in her eyes. "I have found my mirror," he said, lips twisting. "Bright and shining."

His gaze fixed on her hair, and then, not so distant, he looked into her eyes, his gaze transfixing her as he said, "And in its depths I see myself reflected."

She was a good listener, Miss Fairford, his mirror. He began to like that in her above all else. He could not remember a time when Lavinia had ever listened to him so raptly, eyes shining, attention unwavering. He wondered if Stott had won equal attention, wondered how any man, so blessed, could abuse or abandon such attention once it was won.

He confused her with his mention of Medusa and mirrors. He could read that confusion in her eyes, and yet she did not insist upon explanations, saying only, with a serious look and a nod of understanding, "It is good to see oneself clearly."

They found a mirror of another kind in their visit with Miss Nell Blackman, an aging spinster, onetime governess, who lived in a trimly kept cottage on the edge of Barton-on-Heath. She traded loganberry jam for the honey Susan Fairford brought her, and greeted him with a quiet dismissiveness, as if she knew him but a temporary fixture in her friend's life, unimportant in the grand scheme of things.

Miss Fairford spoke to her with quiet fondness, and listened patiently to a stream of trivialities, all of which were of the greatest concern to the old woman. Life was nothing but worries it would seem, a list of troubles to be dealt with. She seemed content in her joylessness. He thought she thrived on the idea of imminent disaster, and he longed to be gone from her company with all haste.

Was such a future what awaited Miss Fairford? A young woman grown old, alone, unhappy, fearful of everything? It troubled him to think so. It stirred him with a desire to in some way change her life before he returned to the troubles of his own, to be sure this need not be her future.

They rode a little farther before he broke the stillness. "You made the suggestion earlier that I might know your misfortunes . . ."

That turned her head, eyes keen, jaw set, lips pressed tight.

"That they involve the mysterious Mr. Stott I would assume, but I know none of the details."

"You need not wait for my disclosure," she said, the downward pull of her mouth bitter. "There are any number who would be pleased to tell you the whole."

"I am sure there are, but gossip is all too unreliable, and if you would prefer I did not hear the truth from your lips, then I need not know the story at all."

She cocked her head to one side, bonnet brim shading the cool blue of her eyes. "I might say the same about you."

"You are a good listener, Miss Fairford. A true friend, to those lucky enough to win your regard. I would be honored to tell you my story one day, if you have any desire to hear it."

"I do."

"And yet, so struck am I by the quality of your concentration in listening to others today, that I would offer you my ear before I bend yours—if you've any wish to be heard."

Clear-eyed, she regarded him from the shadows of her bonnet brim. "A handsome offer, sir."

"Is it?"

She smiled. "You sense my hesitation."

He nodded.

"My reluctance is well founded. You see, a handsome stranger rode into Chipping Campden one day, mounted upon a good horse, fine clothes head to toe, a ready flash of gold from his purse, his manner polite, cordial—well educated."

He cocked his head, listening, wondering if it were he she described.

"He offered me his attentions, his ear. He convinced me I should trust him. Very like you, he was, and yet, I would hope you are nothing like him."

He nodded, afraid to say a word, afraid he might halt her disclosure.

"His name, he claimed, was Theodore William Stott. He owned a prospering business in London. He said he took a cottage in the country in order to escape the summer heat and city stench. He was a liar, Mr. Stone. Just as you are."

She fell silent then, and he did not push her to reveal more, hoping, given time, she would go on.

She tucked away a windblown strand of the glittering copper hair, her expression melancholy.

"I was completely taken in, trusted everything he told me." She hung her head, bonnet brim guarding her features. "His attentions were flattering."

She stroked her hack's mane, as they plodded onward, honey pots jiggling musically. She chewed at her lower lip, frowning, then turned her head, her face a fresh revelation, blue eyes serious, harboring old wounds. "And then he took everything of value from me but Fairford." Her tone had gone defensive, and yet she seemed to realize her position indefensible. She shook her head with a rueful, self-deprecating laugh. "What a fool!"

Gazing sympathetically at a troubled countenance fast becoming dear to him, Philip considered the unforgivably callous and manipulative Mr. Stott, and thought, *What a fool, indeed!*

Chapter Eight

The last of their stops was at the rambling estate of the rejected Sir Gregory Wraxall. More sheep here, and cattle grazing in hock-deep fields of green. The house was in the William and Mary style, red-bricked, with Portland stone quoining and gabled attic. It boasted a formal garden, an orangery and an ice house. Miss Fairford might have been comfortable indeed here, as the respected Lady Wraxhall.

Gregory Wraxall, of all those they visited, questioned Philip the longest, testing the strength of his lies, shaming him with his concern for Miss Fairford.

Balding, paunchy, deeply jowled and tenacious with his inquiry once he sank teeth into it, Sir Gregory reminded Philip of his mastiff, Jacko, a dog he loved dearly despite age and ugliness—a dog he had left behind him, along with everything else, his life entrusted temporarily to the care of others.

He thought they might have been friends, he and Sir Gregory, had they met under any other circumstances, but that he came in Miss Fairford's company as the unknown, and none too forthcoming Mr. Stone, earned him a very stiff-rumped welcome.

He could not blame the old gentleman. Mr. Stone deserved no great welcome, after all. He was a liar, as much as Mr. Stott had been. Wraxall had good instincts.

"Do I know you, sir?" he asked when they were introduced, squinting at Philip, head cocked to one side. "Stone, Stone. I do not recall the name, but I never forget a face, sir, and yours is uncannily familiar. Where is it you say you come from?"

"Dorset, sir."

"Where exactly in Dorset?"

It was not the first time today he had been asked. "Poole," he said. He had actually been to Poole. One could not be involved in shipping and not know Poole.

"Ah. Excellent harbor. Many's the time I have taken a bed at the Angel. You are involved in shipping? Perhaps it is thus I know you. I have had my share of shipping the local wool to the Continent and beyond."

Oh, dear! Philip thought. This was what he had been dreading all afternoon—encountering someone who would think to ask all the wrong questions.

"I have it!" Wraxall slapped his thigh. "By God, I have it. You are the spitting image of a gentleman I once knew, now long dead. What was his name? Chil—No, Chal-something."

Philip sat forward in alarm, immediately regretting his reaction, for Miss Fairford took note.

"Devil take it, why can I not remember?" The old gent rubbed a hand through hair that had taken far too many such assaults, and Philip, astounded that the man had known, even met his father, longed to blurt out his name in assistance, longed to ask under what circumstances the two had known each other.

"A marquess he was,". Wraxall muttered, slapping his thigh again, as if to whip the memory into his mind.

Miss Fairford, whose gaze had bounced from one to the other of them like a shuttlecock in motion, froze in looking at him, lips parting on breath. Philip wondered if she remembered in that instant the initial C on his coin purse.

"Marquess of Chal . . . Chal—"

"—mondeley." He finished it. He could bear the older man's struggle no longer.

"By Jove, that's it, young man! Chalmondeley. How could I forget? Decent chap he was that time we met."

"How did you know?" Miss Fairford asked quietly.

Philip regretted the timing of her interruption, regretted the piercing nature of her look even more. She suspected. She was not a woman easily fooled—not since Stott, not since he had given himself away with the damned coin purse.

He met her gaze without flinching. "It is not the first time I have been told of the likeness," he admitted. It was the truth. One had only to look at the portraits at Rockforth Hall to agree he bore a striking resemblance to his dear, departed father.

"And have you met the likes of the man himself?" Wraxall wanted to know.

"On more than one occasion," Philip admitted quietly. "He was, as you said, a decent chap."

"Decent as they come." Wraxall said it emphatically. "Would that we might say the same of all men, aye, Miss Fairford?"

"Aye," she agreed.

Susan watched the interaction of the two men as though from a great distance, with a strangely comfortable emotional detachment, and the knowing sense that she was not at all the foolish young woman who had once examined through passion-blinded eyes the same sort of exchange between Wraxall and the ever smiling Mr. Stott.

She had believed Sir Gregory Wraxall nothing more than a stuffy old man then, a dear friend of her father's, no longer moved by the fire and verve of youth. She knew him differently now, valued him differently, beloved old fellow.

And Mr. Stone? Or was it Chalmondeley? Whatever his name, the gentleman was a puzzle. She knew he was not to be trusted. She had yet to make up her mind whether he was to be in any way esteemed. She saw wisdom in her own deliberate, unhurried lack of judgment. Stott had given her, in taking almost everything of value from her, the gift of wisdom, maturity and temperance of emotion.

"Thank you for the honey, Susan," Sir Gregory said, taking her hand and tucking it into his arm as he led her into the courtyard, where Mr. Stone saw to the fetching of the horses. "A pleasure to meet your new tenant." He gave her a piercing look. "You have been careful to ascertain he is not another Mr. Stott, have you not, my dear?"

She nodded and gave his arm a pat. "Never fear, dear sir. I am not so foolish now as I was then. I have my eye on Mr. Stone, and know him for what he is."

Wraxall gave a phlegmy chuckle. "And what is he, my dear?"

"A man," she exclaimed, as if that said all.

"What sort of man, be the question."

"A man not to be trusted."

"Are all men ruined then by Mr. Stott's taint?" he asked sadly.

"Not at all," she said in all seriousness. "I trust you, sir. But I will never so readily trust a liar again."

"As well you shouldn't, my gel, but how do you know Stone is a liar?"

She smiled and patted again his steady arm. "Liar or thief. He has told me as much this afternoon."

The groom led up her hack, then offered her his linked hands to throw her up into the saddle.

"Why keep company with such a man, my dear?" Wraxall hissed in agitation, standing beside the groom that she might lean into his shoulder. "Shall I saddle a horse?"

She settled herself, and as she carefully arranged her skirts, leaned down to murmur with a smile, "Kind of you to offer, sir, but not at all necessary, I do assure

you. We've only to go to David Foster's about a gig,
and then home again."

The gig was of a standard, old-fashioned, single-
horse design, the wheels five foot tall, leaning outward,
the two-seater body of the carriage set high, so that
it took some agility with the aid of the iron rung to
fling oneself into it. Not especially smart, but Philip
thought it would do nicely for the few weeks he would
need it.

"My wife is troubled by the rheumatism," Foster
told them. "She has a wee bit of trouble getting in
and out, but it should be no great feat for you, Mr.
Stone, young and fit as you are."

The springs were a C curve configuration, the
weatherproof leather calash looked dry, but the traces
and shafts were in good condition, the wheels and
body bright with a fresh coat of green paint, and there
was a boot box built beneath the seat. Philip thought
it would do nicely.

"Do you think Standard will pull it?" Miss Fairford
asked, voicing the very question on his mind.

Mr. Foster assured him, "Any horse with half a
brain and an even temperament can pull this gig without a problem. But"—he held up his hand in a warning gesture—"if he has a tendency to have his head,
or take the bit between his teeth, then you must not
put him to it. All it takes is a stumble, the shafts hit
the road, and you are tipped out and into the ditch
or onto your head. That is the problem with a one-
horse gig. Makes my wife nervous, it does."

Philip loosed the girth and slid the saddle from the
dun's back. "He is canny enough. We've only to see
if he is willing."

And so Philip carefully put Standard into the traces,
and when it was seen he made no objection to a quick
jaunt about the yard, Mr. Foster stepped down and

offered his hand to Susan that she might mount the high step.

"Do you mind if we test the horse as far as the Rollrights, Mr. Foster?" she asked before lifting her skirt. "We mean to stop for a picnic. I am sure Mr. Stone will have an answer for you on buying the gig by the time we return."

"Aye. Fine with me," he said. "I shall look for you in about an hour then?"

"That would be very kind." She grasped his hand and lifted her skirt to step into the gig.

It was a trifle disconcerting to look up and see Mr. Stone's eyes fix briefly on her exposed ankles, even more so to discover that the gig's seat was very narrow. They could not sit beside each other in it without bumping shoulders.

Shoulder to shoulder, they trotted out of Long Compton. Philip had promised himself he would never again fall prey to the physical lure of a woman, and yet his tongue ceased to work when their elbows banged, when his arm, in guiding the horse, chanced to meet hers.

She sat rigidly, face hidden by the brim of her bonnet, as speechless as he.

As they neared the lane, he must speak in order to ask, "Which way?"

She pointed south, adjusting her position as she did so, arranging her limbs a fraction of an inch farther from his. Her continued silence made it easier for him to speak. "Do you mean to tell me what or who these Rollrights are?" he asked.

"Stones, Mr. Stone," she said coolly. "The locals believe them to be enchanted."

Chapter Nine

Just south of Compton, he saw them, a ring of men hunched in the grass, evergreens screening them from the neighboring fields. On closer examination the men became stones, scoured and pitted by weather and time, a haphazard collection of odd-sized and shaped rocks carefully arranged in a circle.

He drew the gig to a halt in the shade. "Very old, are they?"

"Ancient. Not so impressive as your Avebury or Stonehenge, I'm told, but of local interest."

His Avebury or Stonehenge? Ah, yes. He had said he was from Dorset. That was the trouble with lies. One must keep track of them.

Regretting he had begun their relationship with so many untruths, no better than Lavinia, he loosed Standard from the gig, and she the hack tied at the back, that the horses might graze, for the stones stood knee deep in good grass.

She took up the top blanket from beneath the hack's saddle and one of the honey baskets full of plunder. Plunging ahead of him, through grass that swayed no less beautifully than her hips, she beat a path to a likely pair of rocks, one low enough to sit upon, the other a suitable height to serve as table.

"Enchanted," he said as he followed, though he did not want to be enchanted by any woman, no matter how lovely her figure. A Siren's call he considered it—

ready to dash him on the rocks of his own reckless-
ness.

"What?" She flung the saddle blanket on top of the
lower of the two chosen rocks and turned to look at
him, nothing so enchanting as her face in sunlight, the
brim of her bonnet shading the cool, assessing blue of
her eyes.

"You said they were enchanted?" Philip, who carried another saddle blanket beneath his arm, the saddlebags that served as picnic hampers across his
shoulder, dropped his blanket on top of hers. A good
thought, the saddle blankets. Her posterior, no matter
how alluring, would have been uncomfortable indeed
on the pockmarked stones without them. She was a
sensible woman, Miss Fairford, a logic and order to
her thinking.

"Witchcraft." She uttered the word without hint of
a smile, but he caught sight of a twinkle in her eyes
as she added the caveat, "So they say."

He squatted to unpack the saddlebags, looking up
at her, haloed in sunlight, a bewitching sight, and he
wondered if all women were capable of conjuring
such spells.

"Local legend has it that an invading army once
gathered here," she said, her voice as enchanting to
his ears as was sight of her to his eyes.

As she spoke, he unfolded the linens he had
brought, linens from Fairford's linen press. They bore
twined S's along their edges.

Sight of them silenced her.

"I hope you do not mind if we use these." He
waved a napkin. "I know they are new, but it did
occur to me they would not be dear to you."

"By all means, we should use them," she said a
trifle too ardently, shaking out the folds of a tablecloth
with vigor, draping it without hesitation atop the table
stone, the curve of her breast, as she did so, enticing.

She seemed anxious to return to her story, rushing

a little the telling of it, the haste of her words shutting off the opportunity he had hoped to gain, by way of the linens, to ask her about Stott.

"It is said the witch came to them here, in this field." She thrust the border of S's deep into the grass, the gesture telling. "To taunt them," she said.

"Taunt them, how?" he asked, regretting now the linens. *Regrets, regrets, so many regrets.* He hoped she did not think he meant to taunt her with twined S's.

She rose abruptly from her task to stretch, one hand bracing the small of her back, the other outstretched, making a pointed circuit of the stones. "The witch chanted her spell to the king who led the invading army, a promise, if you will, that she never intended to keep."

He watched her lithe movement as she spoke, not the hunched and motionless stones she pointed to, and he thought of Lavinia and the promises she had never meant to keep.

Miss Fairfield chanted. " 'If Long Compton thou canst see, King of England shalt thou be.' "

Philip turned, scanning the horizon with a frown. "But one cannot see the village."

"No. There is a long barrow in the way. The witch knew that."

"And so she convinced the army they were defeated before the battle ever began, clever woman," he murmured as he took from the basket paper-wrapped meat pies, and a handful of plums.

She looked at him, brows raised as she sliced into a loaf of bread.

"I do not believe in witches," he said. "And so she must have been, instead, a deviously clever woman." He knew *they* existed. A deviously clever woman had convinced him she loved him, had almost managed to marry him.

He held out a plate, and on it a meat pie and a plum. Miss Fairford took it with a thoughtful look, added slices of bread and cheese and handed it back to him.

"And how would you explain your clever woman changing the men to stone—knights, knaves and king?" she asked.

He offered her the second plate, then handed her silverware and a napkin as he sat beside her on the blanket-padded rock. He wished to look upon her face as he suggested, "And so we sit on the back of a long-suffering knave and eat from the lap of a knight?"

She laughed. He loved the sound of it, loved the way it brightened her face and chased all trace of worry from her features. "Something like that, yes. And there"—she pointed with her fork—"the King stone watches us."

"A pockmarked and defeated-looking monarch if ever there was one," he said. "Do you think he envies us our kidney pie?"

"Mmmm." She smiled, set aside her fork, took off her gloves and lifting the pie in bare hands, bit into it with appreciation. "He ought to. This is delicious. I have been missing Betty's meat pies."

With no more than that she reminded him again of her losses.

They fell silent as he poured them each a cup of sack. He waited until she had dabbed lips with a napkin and reached out for her plum before he swallowed his own tart, juicy mouthful and asked her, "Do you believe in witchery? In enchantments? Will these stones rise up again one day, do you think, and stand, weather-worn knights and knaves again?"

She stood, plum in hand, the breeze stirring her bewitching curls about the brim of her bonnet, sunlight burnishing their color magical. "You are better qualified than I to answer that," she said.

He savored the final bite of sweetness from the plum pit. "Am I? How so?"

She licked her lips, sweet, rose-tinted lips that hovered above the unbroken skin of her rose-cheeked plum. Hers were lips that begged to be enchanted with a kiss, lips that lifted in the arch smile of a very clever woman in saying, "You are yourself enchanted, are you not? Changed from knight—or is it knave?—to Mr. Stone."

Chapter Ten

Laughing, he rose to toss his plum pit in the direction of the evergreens, saying enigmatically, "It is true, I came to you bewitched, rock transformed to stone."

What in heaven's name did he mean? *Rock to stone.* She bit into her plum, puzzling the matter.

He turned back to her, juice stickied fingers to his lips, in which act he seemed embarrassed to be caught. He reached immediately for his napkin, while she tried not to think too much about the juicy pluminess of his lips. She thought too often, and completely against her will and better sensibilities, of those lips—of kisses.

She knew of kisses; after all, Mr. Stott had won her with kisses.

As if Mr. Stone knew her thoughts, he captured her gaze and said, "I begin to believe I might fall prey to another sort of enchantment here."

It unnerved her when he said such things, when she thought of him on far too familiar terms. She had made the mistake of Stott. Was Stone but another?

The wind caught the brim of her bonnet, caught the strands of her hair and played havoc with both. His hat waffled, hair tousled like windblown flax. He did not seem to mind, turning face into the breeze, as if toward a lover's touch, eyes closing, lips curving upward in the smile that never failed to put a hitch in her breathing.

Impatient with herself, with the feelings he stirred, she rapped out irritably, "You speak in riddles, sir—riddles and lies."

He opened his eyes, dark wells beneath the brim of his hat. "You are right," he surprised her in saying. "I am ashamed of it. I would apologize, and clarify. I am not from Dorset. I know nothing of Avebury or Stonehenge. It is Devon and Cornwall's rocky coast-line I am most familiar with, boulder-strewn beaches and stony cliffs arranged not by man's hand, but by the forces of God and Nature. I know intimately"—he paused, watching her, the suggestion of the word hanging between them—"the edge of the earth and the beginning of miles of sea and sky. A different kind of enchantment."

A bee hovered, buzzing, near her ear. She shied away from it, shied from him, as well.

"It sounds beautiful."

"I do hope you will see it one day," he said. "Do you think I might tempt you?"

Far more alarmed by his words than by any bee, she looked away from the distant promise of his eyes. Folding her napkin far more carefully than it merited, she thought of Stott and said coolly, "I do my best to resist temptation, Mr. Stone."

Her fingers, long and elegant, carefully aligned the corners of the napkin, carefully smoothing the folds, creating order. He watched, anticipating her intent when she rose to gather up the remains of their poor feast.

He rose as well, to help her, lifting the tablecloth free of his side of the stone as she caught it up from hers. He helped to fold it, once, twice, and then their folded ends must come together.

"Mr. Stott tempted you," he suggested when their hands and eyes met as much as did the corners of the cloth.

She looked down as she took the tablecloth from him, folding the cloth smaller and smaller into a neat, packable bundle. She ran a finger along the border of her embroidered handiwork, a long hissing line of S's for Stott, like a writhing serpent trapped in the threads.

"It is easy to be deceived by those who make a habit of it," he said, thinking of Lavinia.

"And you?" She handed him the bundle of linen. "Do you make a habit of it, Mr. Stone?"

Her contempt had returned. He did not like to see it in her eyes, nor hear it in the way she pronounced the lie of his name.

"No," he protested.

Her brows arched in disbelief.

She had him on the defensive. He said the first thing that popped into his mind. "I've a Stott of my own."

A harsh bark of laughter erupted from a mouth he longed to sweeten with kisses. "I doubt it," she said scathingly.

He flinched, deeply offended, unwilling to have her regard him so ill. "I do not lie to you now, Miss Fairford."

"There cannot be another so vile as Stott." Her voice was as rigid as her backbone as she walked away.

"Do you believe yourself the only one in this world to have your heart trampled on?" he called after her harshly. "The only one pursued by a fortune hunter? Has your heart gone completely numb to another's pain? If so, then you are right. Stott must have been far worse than my fiancée, for he has ruined you for any connection with another man, even that of friendship."

That got her attention, halting momentarily her wade through the grass.

"Friendship!" She whirled, tendrils of copper whipping her cheek, the swirl of her skirts sending waves through the ripple of green as if her anger were greater than she, unbound by bodily limitations. "Answer me this, Mr. Stone." The blue eyes blazed, sunlight on sapphires. "How many friendships have you begun without trust, without benefit of so much as the other party's name? Tell me this, Mr. Stone, or should I call you my lord Chalmondeley? Did she take everything from you?"

He blinked, regretting his earlier outburst. He had not lost as much as she, it was true.

"No," he admitted quietly. He closed the distance between them, so that they both stood ankle deep in a windblown eddy of green. He could not shout his reply. It must be said quietly. "It was her plan to take everything, of course, but in the end all she made off with was a bit of my honor, pride, self-esteem, and all of my . . ." He almost said love, but it was not true. She had not taken that with her. ". . . willingness to trust," he said at last.

"Heavy losses, indeed," she said, and the blue eyes no longer held contempt or anger. Empathy he met with there, and a comforting sight it was.

Too soon she looked away, and turned, as if to set off once more for the gig.

"My name . . ." He stopped her.

"Yes?" She lifted one hand to shade eyes that seemed to see him clearly for the first time since they had met.

". . . is Philip Randall Chalmondeley."

Her lips parted in surprise. Her eyes, a heaven of blue, opened wide. She smiled, rare sight that it was, and held out her hand to him. "Pleased to meet the real you, Mr. Stone."

They fell into a comfortable silence in reloading the gig, catching up the horses and harnessing Standard. They worked well without words, her logic in returning things to order in perfect tandem with his, their movements a quiet symphony of efficiency. She could almost hear the music in his limbs. He had the appearance of a thoroughbred in motion. She delighted in watching him.

She was honored that he had revealed himself to her, and hoped he might be on the verge of telling her more. She feared speech, on her part, might kill his inclination, and so she remained quietly helpful without questioning his former openness.

It was not until they were on the road again, his hands strong and steady on the reins, their shoulders and elbows bumping with every rut in the road, that he spoke.

"I make bold to ask you, Miss Fairford. What did you want of Stott?"

"Stott? What do you mean, *want* of him?"

"Husband? Lover? Companion? What did you hope—"

"Why do you wish to know?" She cut him short. Why did he touch upon *her* history when it was *his* she wished to know more of.

Voice quiet, he asked, "Has he left you distrustful of all men? Questioning their every motive? Unwilling to open up to strangers?"

Her anger flared. "It is a mistake to be too trusting, too open. There is wisdom to be found in keeping one's own counsel, in not revealing too much of thought or feeling. Are you not circumspect in what you have revealed to me? And for the same reasons?"

"True. It is just—"

"Just what?"

"I wished to know if my own expectations were unrealistic."

So this had less to do with her than with him, after all. She sighed, anger fading. "What expectations?"

He flicked the reins and chirruped to the horse as they bounced from open field onto paved road. His hands on the reins moved with steady, unshakable purpose. As the dust settled and Standard's hooves established a steady rhythm on the macadam, he tipped his head to look in her direction, the breeze playing like a woman's hands in the pale wheat of his hair, pushing it back from the broad expanse of his forehead, tugging at the brim of his hat.

"I desired much of marriage," he said. "I wanted a helpmate, a confidant, fosterer of the best in me, supporter of my dreams and aspirations, a mother for my unborn children."

She tried to imagine what his children would look like, picturing fair-haired lads with windblown forelocks and self-possessed little girls with distant green eyes.

He turned to watch the horse, his voice drifting to her as he spoke to the road ahead. "I expected a woman who would share with me good times and bad, a wife who could recognize the best and worst in me. I expected faithfulness, passion, empathy and companionship. I looked forward to growing old together. Were my hopes too high? I ask you."

Her view of the road blurred. She blinked back tears. Too close this vision to her own idea of marriage's potential.

"I think . . ." She paused. She could not tell him his vision of marriage moved her deeply.

"Yes?" His hat cartwheeled against the sun.

She kept her head bent, the bonnet's brim her straw shield. "I think I am not at all the person to ask when it comes to marital expectations."

"Oh." He flicked the reins impatiently.

"Yes," she admitted. "My union was a complete failure—my hopes and dreams too closely akin to yours to offer any great sense of perspective."

His hands stilled, hovering like her words. "Perhaps you are right."

She did not want to be right, did not want to leave

their discussion concluded so unsatisfactorily. "I sincerely hope your expectations were not too high, Mr. Stone, and I wish you every success in finding such a match."

Chapter Eleven

The sun turned the road golden before them, the uneven surface throwing them together again, shoulder to shoulder, elbow bumping elbow, hip brushing hip. She was not so stiff as before, he noticed. She did not try so hard to hold herself aloof. *This* was what he had expected of marriage—a gentlewoman at his side of like mind and purpose, a female unafraid to debate the most profound of issues, and willing to admit when she had not the answers.

They approached David Foster's courtyard in a silence both companionable and tension fraught. From the moment they had met he had felt this same sense of anticipation whenever they were in close physical proximity, and yet he resisted its pull. He had suffered just such feelings in his infatuation with Lavinia. They were not to be trusted, much less indulged.

Foster called to them as they pulled into the yard before his carriage house. "I see your horse has taken to the gig without a problem, Mr. Stone, Do you like it half so much as he does?"

"I am ready to strike a bargain," Philip replied. As he stepped down from the gig, it occurred to him that marriage, too, was a bargain struck, and that he had been saved from the making of a bad one.

The gig, no honey jars to coddle, allowed them to set off at a much faster rate returning to Chipping Campden than they had achieved in leaving it behind them. They paused too long, however, in fetching the lamb's leg from the Millers, the sun setting in their faces in the last part of their journey. The same birds that had fled their approach that morning settled to roost, muttering and chittering in the trees and shrubberies along the roadside.

They talked of trivialities as the creaking wheels put the miles behind them, all of it surface chatter, like the birds, until the lane went soft with the twilight, and they drew into themselves and their own private thoughts as the horses' hooves ticked away the passing of the sun's remnant glow.

Susan did not mean to lower her guard against the liar sitting beside her, and yet she could not jolt along for hours, forever rigid and wary. It took too much effort, and her body had been wearied by the day, by her constant vigilance, and the sun in her eyes.

That she now knew the secret of Philip Randall Chalmondeley's full and proper name, that he spoke so openly of his feelings with regard to marriage, disarmed her, if not completely, at least enough that she no longer felt compelled to sit completely rigid in the gig, resisting the brush of their shoulders with every dip and rut in the road.

The sky went pink, violet and gold. The coming night smelled of loamy earth and bruised marjoram, darkness seeping across the sky like spilled ink, contentment seeping into her heart in a similar fashion.

It was a relief to relax, lulling. With the setting sun too much gold to look upon, too warm its cloak upon her head and shoulders, the silence between them weighed heavy. It filled her throat, sweet and numbing as a soporific, like a metronome ticking with the rhythmic clopping of the horses' hooves. She fell into a drowsing state, eyelids drooping, head swaying, bobbing, bouncing with the rhythm, falling at last onto the solid and comfortable woolen support of his shoulder.

She woke to find him tucking his greatcoat about

her, the bone and muscle of his shoulder all too solid and warm beneath her cheek.

"Ah, Miss Fairford, I did not mean to wake you," he apologized, his breath warm and faintly plummy against her hair, her scalp, the upper curve of her ear. He smelled of bay leaf cologne. The jacket with which he had covered her gave the fleeting and slightly smothering impression she lay beneath him.

"Oh, my!" She sat up in alarm. "Dropped off, have I? Terribly rude of me. I am sorry."

"No trouble. You've just been taking a wee nap."

She gave his shoulder a nervous pat. "I have not drooled on you, have I? Or snored in your ear? How very embarrassing."

"No drooling, no snoring, no names murmured in your dreams. You've nothing at all to be embarrassed about."

And yet she was. Her cheeks burned with it, hot in the cool of the night. Heat along her neck, too. She was glad there was no light in which her blushing might be witnessed. She was very embarrassed to have relaxed so completely, to have let down her guard.

The gait of his horse had slowed to a walk in the darkness. Her fingertips tingled with the change in temperature, her neck and shoulders stiff from the position she had assumed. *God,* what must he think of her! To have leaned against him so forwardly!

Above her, stars threw a sprinkling of dim light along the gig's leather calash. The moon cut an uneven hole in the sky, and along the edges of the lane there appeared an occasional eerie green glow, a distraction that kept her from spending the rest of their drive berating herself.

"Oh, look!" she gasped. "Glowworms to light the way home! Why did you not wake me? How marvelous!"

"Yes. The ladies are putting on quite a show."

"Ladies? Is it just the females who glow?"

"Indeed. Rather forward young misses from what I have read."

Her cheeks burned afresh. "Forward. How so?"

"It is only their tails that glow. The worm props them in the wind and waits for some susceptible male to come along to play husband to them."

"The male glowworm does not glow?"

"The male glowworm is not a worm at all, but a beetle. He can produce a slight glow, nothing like the showier female, but he lives only to please her, and then does. Rather like the drone bee."

"How sad."

"I prefer to think of it as romantic."

His remark inspired silence, an uneasy, charged stillness broken only by the noise of the wheels on the road, the sound of Standard's shod hooves, and an occasional whiffle or snort from the hack tied behind.

"You find it romantic that the male dies for love?"

"Eminently so."

"You would do as much for a woman?" Her question cut the darkness, sharp as a knife. Her tone held skepticism rather than the admiration most females would have lavished on him for such a remark.

That she did not immediately swallow his every word like sweet honey, indeed, that she challenged him to support, even defend his claims, added a humming edge to the already buzzing level of tension in their every conversation. He found it stimulating—intriguing.

The moonlight on her features revealed teasing glimpses of face and feeling, a peek at her chin and nose, the line of her lips. Though she sat right beside him, her eyes were hidden, entirely overshadowed by bonnet brim and the gig's calash. He longed at times for light, that he might more accurately gauge her reaction.

Her interest in their conversation, even when they

discussed nothing more important than insects and her vehemence in supporting her opinions, impressed him with her afresh.

He had thought of Lavinia as he detailed the behavior of the glowworm. She had undoubtedly waved her brightness before him to catch his eye. Not Miss Fairford, though her hair outshone Lavinia's by far. She did not tempt him with her beauty. She did not agree with his every word. Was he more drone to her queen bee than beetle to glowworm? Must he fly higher and faster to win her approval?

"For true love," he said carefully, knowing he had gained a clearer idea of what true love really was that very day, "I would give my life gladly."

She heaved a sigh, as if his answer in some way disgusted her. "I can only hope your love is never put to such a tragic test."

"Why? Do you doubt me?"

"Are you the sort of man who, drawn to the glitter of a woman, would throw everything over for her, no matter the risk? I have known such men, drawn or repelled for no more reason than the transient light of beauty, be it the color of a woman's hair or the cast of her countenance."

He knew in that instant that she spoke of herself, of her glorious, eye-catching hair.

"Cut off the hair, lose or scar the beautiful countenance, and the woman is essentially unchanged. Her soul, her love, her inner being is the same, but the man, confused, does not recognize her, or value her, without the light that drew him."

Lavinia.

"Tell me," he said, voice soft, on the edge of anger, "what does a man do when he is ready to die for a woman, ready to play the drone, the short-lived glowworm beetle, but . . . the light of the soul he thought he knew, the light of love and inner beauty that lured him to the brink of his very existence, proves false, deceitful, nothing but a sham?"

A silence fell between them before she said quietly, "He must seek the true light—a worthy woman of fortitude, independence and wisdom."

"Why? That the beetle's short life need not be wasted?"

"No." She laughed. "I must admit I did not consider his loss so much as hers. You see, if his life is spent, she will be left alone—to support and raise her brood, to grow old and die—alone. A feat that requires great fortitude and independence, think you not?"

"And wisdom?"

"Yes." She laughed ruefully, then said with a bitterness that increased with every word, "Wisdom enough not to lose her inheritance to the first sweet-talking fortune-hunting bug who would crawl her way."

Chapter Twelve

The darkness was complete when they drove into the lamplit closeness of Chipping Campden, the air redolent with the smell of roasting potatoes, lamb chops, and cabbage. Mr. Stone, she still thought of him as such, delivered her to her front step.

Curtains parted at the window next door, lamplight gleaming, as nosy Mrs. Whorley took stock of their arrival. There was no mistaking her frizzled, mob-capped head.

Philip made quick work of helping Susan down. Together they unloaded her things.

"I shall see your hack is returned, shall I?" he asked as he plucked up the leg of lamb as if it weighed no more than a feather, and ducking his head to clear the doorway, carried it inside her cottage.

She preceded him, carrying one of the loaded baskets, self-conscious of the cramped proportions of the parlor, showing him the niche in the larder where meat sometimes hung, when she had an abundance of it—a luxury she could not often claim.

He turned quickly from his task, far quicker than she expected, quick enough to run into her as he turned from the darkness into the light of the lamp she had just lit. He caught her shoulder with a mild exclamation of surprise, steadying her, steadying the lamp between them.

She, fearful she might drop it otherwise, let him.

His eyes flashed wide. The lamplight, reflected

there, leapt in a tiny, silvered green flame. Her cheeks burned. The warm weight of his fingers seemed to sear through the fabric of her sleeve, tindering a conflagration deep within her—the heat of wanting, of desire. Her lips, hot and dry, were in need of quenching.

They stood thus, a moment too long, she thought, and yet she could not move nor break away her gaze until he said, "Beg pardon," and stepped back.

"No harm done," she murmured, lowering the lamp, the lie sticking in her throat. He had achieved in an instant what she had fought against all day. With no more than a firm grasp upon the very shoulder that had rubbed against his all afternoon, the shoulder he had wrapped in his own coat, he lit the banked coals of a desire she had done everything to extinguish.

"It was a lovely day," he said, voice low, his lamplit gaze as stimulating as his touch.

"Fine weather," she agreed, the words thick as treacle, catching in her throat. She set the lamp beside her on the table and shrugged his coat away from her shoulders.

As she did so, he stepped in behind her, his hands on the lapel, helping in the undressing of her.

"I enjoy your company," he said.

"I enjoyed the use of your coat," she said, swaying against him, trapped fast in the sleeves. The coat was finely tailored, the arms closely shaped. It clung to her like a lover.

Philip turned her, as a valet would, by the shoulders, one hand running the length of the sleeve to tug at the cuff, the other meeting hers at the wrist. She looked up.

He wanted to kiss her. She could read desire in the smoldering gleam of his eyes, in the fresh tilt to his chin, in the slight unevenness of his breathing as he stopped his attempts to slide the coat free.

His mouth rearranged itself.

"A tight fit," he said.

She held her breath, wishing he would kiss her, dizzy with wishing, breathless. She had to remind herself to breathe. Her bosom rose on the depth of her inhalation. Her lips parted.

He leaned closer, the bulk of his body blotting the lamplight. His breath rifled her hair. She tipped up her chin, knowing he would kiss her, wanting it.

He refrained, choosing instead to try a fresh tactic, pulling the coat back about her shoulders, smoothing the fabric along her arms. He reached again for her wrist. "It is thus my valet always manages to remove it successfully," he said, and indeed, when he tugged at the cuff this time, it slid easily over her fingertips.

She withdrew her arm. The coat, unbalanced, slid its freed arm provocatively down across her hip.

The heat of his breath, smelling faintly of honey and plums, fanned across her nose and heated the sensitive surfaces of her lips as he leaned forward to catch up the other shoulder of the coat with one hand, the cuff with the other.

She shivered as he tugged the fabric free, as the last remnant of his warmth slipped away. She closed her eyes, regretting the loss, opening them to find him frozen, the coat suspended forgotten in his hands, his attention fixed on her face, her eyes, her lips.

Her own attention strayed to his mouth. Of all the things Mr. Stott had taught her, she liked the bliss of kissing best. As if he read her mind, Philip—she dared to think of him as Philip—stepped closer, the coat dropping forgotten from hands intent on clasping her waist, on drawing her close.

His lips hovered. The air hummed with potential between them. She closed her eyes, expecting the perfect end to a perfect day.

"Coo-wee!" came a call from the front step. "Home at last, are you, Suz?"

They flew apart like startled birds, the moment shattered.

"Mrs. Whorley, my neighbor." She whirled to greet the woman, who in an instant darkened the open doorway.

Philip caught up the lantern, its sudden rise from the table throwing uneven shadows upon the wall, erratic as her heartbeat as he murmured, "I shall just go and fetch that last basket, shall I?"

"Yes, please," she agreed breathlessly, following him to the door, Mrs. Whorley stepping aside to let him pass.

As the night swallowed him up, Mrs. Whorley addressed Susan in a querulous undervoice, as if she had important secrets to tell. "Vicar's been by."

"Has he?" Susan asked calmly.

Her mobcapped head bobbed. "He asked if you had returned. I told him I did not think you had, for surely I would have heard some noise from the horses. And it is just as I said. I could not help but hear the wheels of the gig!"

Susan stepped into the night, to cool her cheeks, to watch Philip Chalmondeley return to her, to escape in some way Mrs. Whorley's all too prying interest.

The woman followed at her heels, calling out to the gentleman she knew as Stone, "And so you have decided to take Mr. Foster's gig after all, despite his tumble into the ditch with it."

Like a light, Philip Chalmondeley's face emerged from the darkness of the street, basket in hand, brows arched. "Ditch?" he managed to ask as he bore the basket into the cottage, before Mrs. Whorley, who followed him, started to explain.

"Never you mind that. He has been good enough to repaint it, has he not? I am sure it looks no worse for the wear by the light of day. Drinks, on occasion, he does, David Foster. I should not wonder that he had had one too many when the gig overturned, though he would blame it on the horse."

"Yes." Philip Stone wore an uncomfortable look.

"Well, I shall take my leave of you now, Miss Fairford, Mrs. Whorley. I shall take the hack with me, shall I? To stable him at Fairford. The stable lad can return him in the morning."

"If you please," Susan said.

Mrs. Whorley was not above following them to the door as they said their good-byes.

"It smells like rain," Philip said, his face lifted to the breeze.

"Yes, you have been fortunate in the weather," Mrs. Whorley said, as if the remark had been directed at her. "Or unfortunate, depending on your point of view. We could not blame your tardiness on rain. Vicar did suggest you might have lost a wheel, or the horse might have gone lame." She stifled a laugh. "We had begun to wonder if we should send a search party out after you, but I told Vicar, I did, that we need do no such thing, that it was no wonder two young people should dawdle a bit on such a day in such delightful weather. I was young once, too, I told him. Nothing like a drive in the fresh air, down a quiet back lane when one is young."

Philip did not hesitate in throwing a wide-eyed look of innocence their way as he stepped up into the gig.

"We stayed too long at the Millers," Susan felt the need to explain.

"We did dawdle a bit on the way home, too," Philip admitted with a contagious smile for Mrs. Whorley that had her grinning vapidly back at him. "There were ladies, you see, with little green lanterns to light the way, and I've a great fondness for"—his eyes narrowed mischievously as he raised the reins—"etymology."

The gig lurched into motion.

"Etta . . . who?" Mrs. Whorley eyed Susan askance.

Susan stifled a laugh. "Mology," she said.

"I do not know her," Mrs. Whorley declared, walking back into Susan's cottage as if she had been invited.

It was, of course, Mrs. Whorley who found Philip Chalmondeley's coat where it had dropped, and bending, shook it out and asked, "What's this doing in a heap on the floor, then?"

"Oh, dear!" Susan exclaimed. "That is Mr. Stone's. I shall just run down the lane and return it."

Snatching up the coat, she paid no mind to Mrs. Whorley's sensible admonition. "If he saw fit to remove it, he is not so chilled that he will need it before morning, my dear."

Susan did not want to hear her. She did not want to behave sensibly. What she wanted was one more uninterrupted moment in Mr. Stone's company. Tonight, before the light of day drove enough sense into her brain to remind her that she must not listen to her heart, to remind her what trouble her last yearning for kisses had gotten her into.

She half ran along the road to Fairford, arriving breathless and winded, and all too foolishly hopeful. She stopped at the tree line in the darkness, pausing to collect herself a little, to ascertain whether Mr. Chalmondeley-Stone had already gone into the house, or if he remained, as she might expect, in the stables.

In answer to her question, the stable door threw a golden square of light into the darkness, and out Philip stepped, his hair lit like a halo. He called instructions to the stable boy over his shoulder.

Susan took a deep, steadying breath and would have stepped out of the shadows to meet him, had not the front door to Fairford Manor swung wide in that instant, the silhouette of a gentleman blotting the light from inside.

"My lord," he called.

Susan froze. *My lord.* Just as Sir Gregory had come so close to guessing.

"Mr. Dover?" Philip's voice seemed suddenly that of a stranger. "Is that your team of bays, then?"

"Yes, my lord."

"How nice to see you. I did wonder who in the world might be visiting me. So few know of my whereabouts."

Susan turned uncertainly, the coat clutched in her hands. She ought not stay and eavesdrop. And yet, she was tempted. Had she but known a little more about Mr. Stott she would never have made the mistake of marrying him.

"I wish it were a friendly visit brought me here, my lord, rather than the business at hand."

"Is something wrong to bring you all the way from London?"

The gentleman came down the steps. The two men met in the middle of the courtyard, their voices dropping. Susan could hear little of what was said.

". . . had to come. Best not entrusted to the post."

"News?" Philip's voice, since he faced her, carried better.

"You must . . . , my lord," was all the response she caught.

"London? Whatever for?"

A name, he said, something that started with an L? The rest she could not make out at all.

Philip's angry response was easier understood. "*She* would charge *me*?"

They moved together toward the house. In turning, she could now hear the stranger better.

"Poor timing, my lord." He shook his head sadly. "To breach promise on the day of the wedding."

"I had good reason." Philip's response was loud and clipped, and then, quietly, he said something about money, ending with an irritable "Can we not settle this thing?"

Susan, aghast, unwilling to hear more, turned to go, but her shock was not yet complete.

"She claims she is with child."

There was no mistaking what had been said. The words rang out clearly, the stranger's voice carrying from the well of the entryway as the two men stepped inside. With no chance to hear Philip Randall Chalmondeley's response, the door closed softly behind them.

She was left with the noises of the night and the echo in her mind of those horrible words.

She claims she is with child.

As if heaven objected, it began to rain.

Chapter Thirteen

Susan was wakened the following morning by a furious banging on her front door and a pelting noise against her windows, as if someone meant to beat the cottage from all sides at once, and the sun not yet up—an awful sound.

She was, in an instant, returned to the days following her wedding when she had awakened more than once to just such a noise from the local tradesmen, come to demand payment on Mr. Stott's expenditures.

Mr. Burdock, the tapman from the Red Lion, had come more than once before the sun was up. She would never forget the lecherous gleam in his eyes when she came running down the stairs in her nightclothes the morning after her wedding night, certain the house was on fire, or worse. She had gone to bed alone, woken to find the pillow empty beside hers, the bed cold where her new husband should have lain.

She rose swiftly, wrapping herself in quilted camisole, feet tucked into bedside slippers. The pounding continued, joined now by an angry male voice calling her name in a none too friendly manner.

A quick glance at the mantel clock revealed the morning more advanced than she had thought, the absence of sun due to overcast skies and the splattering of rain.

"Where is your husband, Mrs. Stott?" Burdock had demanded that fateful morning. "Word has it he slipped town last night with your horses. The noise of their passing woke my sister."

He had known before she had! His sister, too, and his wife, plus whosoever they might have told. She still flushed with embarrassment at the memory.

Not Mr. Burdock, this morning. Mr. Jenks waited upon the doorstep, and he looked no more pleased with her than with the weather that plastered his hair to his forehead.

"Where's mah horse?" he demanded as soon as she swung wide the door, no interest at all in her disheveled state except perhaps as an additional source of irritation. His face was livid, his voice burly with impatience. "You did promise to return him to me before sundown."

"Has not Mr. Stone returned him to you?" she asked calmly, though within her breast rose a familiar panic. Had Philip Randall Chalmondeley abandoned her, taking with him the horse, just as Stott had?

"Stone? I've no business with Stone. It is you I had an agreement with. The animal would be safely returned to me, you said yesterday," Jenks railed.

"Yes, Mr. Jenks. I do apologize. Mr. Stone left me last night with the understanding he would return the horse to you. It was a little after sundown by the time we returned."

"And me already in bed if he did try to return the beast. I do rise early, you know, and we've no money to be wasting on candles."

"No, of course. Your horse should be safely housed and fed in the stables at Fairford if he has not been returned to you. Will you walk with me there, as soon as I am properly dressed?"

"I will not, Miss Fairford. I've neither time nor temperament to be hanging about waiting for a woman who should already be up and dressed, and I've no inclination to go traipsing about in the rain after my own beast that should already have been returned to me."

"No. Of course not. I do beg your pardon for his tardy return. I shall see about fetching him immediately."

She did not linger over her toilet, and within a quarter of an hour stood, bonnet dripping, upon the steps of dear old Fairford Manor, Lord Chalmondeley's forgotten jacket tucked safely beneath the damp overhang of her cloak. Feeling quite bedraggled and not at all anxious to see Lord Chalmondeley, she studied the door knocker as she waited. It was a ram's head, his nose shiny with wear, the curl of his great horns burnished, too, from years of rapping the solid English oak.

In this same spot a stranger had turned to Philip Chalmondeley with the terrible words she could not forget.

She claims she is with child.

She thought of Mr. Stott as she waited, and she thought of the woman with child who had been abandoned. Her anger rose, encompassing both men, Stott and Stone, two beguiling liars who would break their commitments—breach their promises. With increasing vigor she rapped the ram's head.

Perry opened the door, looking greyer than she remembered in the morning light, and yet not a hair out of place. His manner was, as always, polite and soothing, his gaze warm in regarding her.

"Miss Susan." He opened the door wide that she might step in out of the rain. The house had a feeling of emptiness, their voices echoed in the stone-floored stairwell. "Is it Mr. Stone you are wanting so early in the morning, Miss?"

"Actually it is Lord Chalmondeley I would speak to," she muttered darkly.

His brow knit in confusion. "Was not the gentleman's name Dover?" he asked carefully.

"Unless *he* is a liar as well." Her comment further provoked the pucker between his brows.

"Miss?"

She sighed and flung open her cloak, pulling forth the coat. "Mr. Stone left this at my cottage yesterday. I wished to return it, and to find out what he has done with Mr. Jenks's hack."

"I am happy to take the coat, marm, but I've no knowledge of the hack. Stone is gone."

"Gone?" A hint of panic welled within her.

He nodded placidly. "You have just missed them. It was the other gentleman's coach they took. What did you say his name was?"

"Gone where?"

"London, miss."

"Does he mean to return?"

"Mr. Stone?" The idea seemed not to have occurred to him. "He gave me no impression he would not. In a devilish hurry, he was. He expressed no desire I should accompany him, and I could not help overhearing that he seemed not at all happy to be going."

Philip scowled at his rain-drenched window to an overcast countryside, the team, the wheels of the coach spattering dabs of mud on the glass, their rumble and splash-filled progress almost as loud as the pounding noise his pulse made in his ears. His blistering rage had returned, his blood throbbed in neck and wrist. *Lavinia! Pox on the woman.* How dare she bring suit!

"My lord?" The solicitor's sober face reflected in the pane was as unpromising as the view.

"Mmmm?" Philip grunted. He had gotten little rest, his mind preoccupied with the mess Lavinia would make of his life.

"You are certain, my lord?"

"Of what, Mr. Dover?"

Dover sat forward, his manner anxious. "This rift between you and your intended."

Philip closed his eyes and leaned his head back against the squabs.

"Can it not be mended?" Dover went on. "Is marriage out of the question, my lord? Your brother—"

Philip sat forward abruptly, his movement silencing Dover. "My brother? What about my brother?"

"He has tried to reach you, my lord, through our offices."

"You did not reveal my whereabouts?"

"No, my lord. We were under strict orders to tell no one. We told him as much." He drew from his pocket a folded square of paper bearing the family seal. "He asked us to forward this to you."

Philip regarded the letter as if it were an adder, poised to strike.

"I've no desire to see it." Without so much as touching it, he closed his eyes and leaned back, insisting acerbically, "Let us be perfectly clear about two things, Mr. Dover. Lavinia Keck is the last woman on earth I might ever be induced to wed, and my brother has nothing to say to me that I would care to hear. We are estranged."

Susan hurried, without actually running. It would not do to be seen running from the house to the stables, afraid of what she would find, or not find. The fear echoed another day's. She had run to the stables that morning, still clad only in her nightgown and quilted chemise, to find the horses gone, every one of them, the stalls standing open, vacated, from carriage horses to riding mare. Seven old friends taken from her in the night, valued by her new husband as she had been valued—for what they might bring him in the way of coin.

Through the doors she burst. Standard snorted and raised his head in alarm, ears pricked, muscles tensed, walleyed. A troubled whickering noise issued from his throat.

She skidded to a halt, soothing words tumbling—relieved—oh so relieved. She stopped to catch her breath and still the pounding of her pulse, letting the fear that had driven her here subside.

Philip Chalmondeley meant to return. He would never leave such a valuable horse behind if he did not mean to return.

But—her eyes widened—Mr. Jenk's hack was nowhere to be seen!

Calmer now, she whirled on her heel, striding outside and around the stables to the pasture where the horses were allowed to graze.

No hack. No groomsman to be seen. No stable lad.

They could not have all gone to London with him. Someone must have been left behind to see to Standard.

Fretting over how she was ever to pay Mr. Jenks for the missing horse, she strode once more through the stables, checking the tack room and lad's quarters. On her way out she encountered the groom, just running in from the wet, coat sodden, cap dripping.

"Freddie," she called.

As he removed the cap, he looked up surprised. "Yes, miss?"

"Mr. Jenks's horse? Do you know what's become of it?"

Freddie looked concerned. "Are you needin' the beast, marm? If so, I am sorry. Just returned it to Mr. Jenks, I did. The last thing Mr. Stone said to me before he left was that I must be sure and see to it, miss."

It was not until after they had stopped for a change of horses that Dover dared question Philip again. He timed it well, waiting until their bellies were full, their thirsts quenched. He did not speak until the posting housekeeper's wife stepped into view, a mewling babe at her shoulder. It was only then he dared ask stiffly, "And the child, my lord?"

Philip tried to picture Lavinia soothing her babe, raising it with a smile to her shoulder, humming a song beneath her breath, as the woman before him did. He sighed. He did not think Lavinia had it in her. A wet nurse must soothe Lavinia's brat, he was sure of it.

Philip almost blurted out, "I will not take to wife another man's mistress, any more than I will claim as heir another man's bastard." But he bit back the words.

What he said was, "The child is none of my concern."

Chapter Fourteen

Philip arrived in London, the skies as grey as his mood, and still he had not told Mr. Dover what needed to be said.

Lodged at the White Hart, he met with his solicitor again the following day at his offices, a quietly productive sort of place, the walls lined with files and bookcases, halls and nooklike offices busy with whey-faced secretaries. They all seemed to be tall, lean, serious-looking lads whose quick, purposeful movements, hushed voices and omnipresent scratch and clink of pen to inkwell impressed the visitor immediately with the important nature of their business. Philip was reminded of Miss Fairford's beehives.

Dover appeared as he entrusted his hat and coat to a bespectacled lad as dour as any undertaker. The lad was sent for coffee while Dover led Philip through the rabbit's warren of offices to a door marked PRITNEY on a polished brass plate.

Pritney, heavily whiskered, a weighty man given to weighty remarks, held court behind a gleaming walnut desk heavily carved with swans and icanthus leaves. Watts, the second partner in the triumvirate, rose, spectacles gleaming in the lamplight, the seriousness with which they regarded his case brought home to Philip by the partners' united presence.

Muted greetings were made. The grim-faced secretary appeared with a tray, cups and coffee, pouring for everyone but himself. He politely doled out lumps of sugar and dribbles of cream before settling at a stool beside the desk. Then he took up his pen, and in clinking it into the inkwell, effectively called their little meeting to order.

It seemed suddenly a darkly paneled, rainy, windowed room full of aged and respectable gentlemen and an undertaker's assistant, all trying to convince Lord Rockforth to do the right thing.

The partners deemed the right thing a marriage and nothing less. Philip deemed it something else. And in so doing, he chose not to reveal the whole of his situation. He hoped they need never know. He hoped the melancholy secretary and his scratching pen, like a wagging tongue, need never make a permanent record of his true shame, pain and sense of betrayal.

He did not blame them for trying to arrange his life. He simply and politely refused to bow to their wishes. A sense of proportion kept him mum.

Was it best, after all, for the parties concerned, that he confess? Was it best the world knew what had truly transpired? After all, it was not confession Lavinia desired of him, just money. He was willing enough to pay for his poor judgment. He was more than willing to allow her the freedom to live with her choices as long as they no longer included him.

Recognizing his entrenched position, the solicitors kept further opinion to themselves and dutifully bent their heads to the task of determining what financial settlement might be made.

"Is there a ceiling on the amount beyond which you will not negotiate?" Mr. Pritney asked, templing his fingers.

The sad-eyed secretary waited, pen poised.

Philip named a sum.

Watts gasped. Pritney's templed fingers flew apart.

Dover had already heard mention of the sum and had already made his objections on the road to London. He sat resigned and silent.

"Too great a settlement, my lord," Mr. Pritney warned. "Declares you a guilty man."

"Payment cannot make an innocent man guilty," Philip objected with a bitter laugh.

"It is the implication of guilt we speak of here, my lord," Watts rushed to explain. "Such a sum cannot but enflame public opinion. There are those who would judge you generous fool, and those who would think you suffering a guilty conscience given word of such an amount. They will require no truth, no proof."

Outside, the rain fell heavier, a thunder on the roof above, an assault on the windowpanes.

Philip sat back, studying them as they studied him, and he knew they were right, that they themselves judged him. "I will not back down," he said. "Write a contingency into the agreement if you like. She must not discuss the settlement with anyone, or risk losing it."

"But my lord!"

He knew as well as they did that one could not stop gossip with contingencies.

"A woman in her condition will not be ignored," Pritney pointed out.

Philip was in no mood for argument. "Given enough money, Lavinia may marry another before her state becomes too pressing—too obvious."

That silenced them. It was not a friendly silence. Their eyes reminded him of the rain on the windows— chill, unpromising.

"And the child, my lord?" Watts asked flatly.

"What about the child?" Philip kept his emotions in check.

"Is allowance to be paid for the child's upkeep?"

"No. She must apply to another for that."

The chill looks grew frostier still.

He rose to go. "You will see everything arranged to my satisfaction?" he asked flatly.

They shoved back their chairs, making polite promises to do as he said, their contempt of him well masked.

It did not matter what they thought. He bowed and wished them good day.

Dover, ever the professional, followed him out. "We will keep you informed as to her solicitor's responses."

Philip shrugged on his greatcoat. The dour secretary offered assistance, hovering.

"You wished to ask me something else?" Philip inquired.

"Yes, my lord." Dover made a dismissive gesture. The secretary bowed cheerlessly and left them. Dover leaned close to whisper, "Can the young lady be trusted not to reveal too soon the details of your settlement, my lord?"

Philip thrust his hands into his coat pockets, grimly considering what Lavinia might do.

He extracted kid gloves from the coat pockets, soft as Miss Fairford's hands. Smoothing them on, he thought of their day together with the faintest of smiles. He flexed his fingers. Had the question been put to him about Miss Fairford, he might have immediately answered. She was as tight-lipped as a woman could be. But Lavinia?

"You assume I knew the young woman more intimately than I do, Mr. Dover. I've no idea how she will respond."

"No idea?"

And she was to marry you? Philip could almost hear the thought voiced.

"I was too blinded by infatuation to see her clearly," he said. He could not tell the man he had assumed Lavinia thought as he did, that she would react as he did, that she had loved him at least as much as she claimed to. Must he come right out and call her deceptive? And himself a naive fool?

"I see," Dover said, faintly skeptical.

Philip knew he did not *see*. How could one *see* when ignorant of half the facts?

"Ah, a man of vision," he said in bitter jest, knowing Dover's ignorance, and growing ill opinion of him, was his own doing. "I would guess then you could tell me how to *see* about tracking someone down who might not care to be found."

"Who, my lord?"

Philip donned his hat and tapped it firmly into place.

"A cunning liar who once went by the name of Stott."

Susan assumed the duties of housekeeper. It made no sense to hire anyone else when she was not sure Lord Rockforth—she must get used to thinking of the lying scoundrel as such—meant to return for any reason other than to fetch his horse.

She found herself enjoying the task. It was as if, briefly, she were mistress of Fairford Manor again, as she drifted daily through its rooms, ordering them cleaned, swept and polished. Reality must be remembered only in the evenings when she returned to the little cottage she leased in the High Street, when she came face-to-face with the reality that she was now responsible for the condition of two houses.

Exhausted, she sank into the uncomfortable concavity of her bed, wondering once again how much the local smithy would ask of her to add additional slats to the bed frame. She regarded the water stain on the ceiling.

A letter had come from Mr. Stone.

The stain was in the shape of Italy, a country that had always fascinated her as a child when her father spoke of his grand tour. She had imagined him a young man, a froth of lace at wrist and neck, a black patch beside his mouth, feathered hat upon his head.

He had spoken to her of Venice, of Rome, of palaces, museums and ruins. She had pictured herself going there on her honeymoon. Stott had promised that she should. There seemed small chance of it now.

She wondered if Lord Rockforth had ever strolled the Colosseum, if he had pursued Latin conquests in a gondola. His letter was brief—businesslike. It detailed his whereabouts in London should she need to reach him. It indicated that urgent business had called him away, a business that might keep him in London indefinitely, a business that could not be concluded without his participation. She wondered if he was even greater scoundrel than Stott had been, if his business had to do with a young woman he spurned and left with child.

She rolled over on the bed, unwilling to look at the ceiling any longer. She wondered if she might one day feel inclined to thank Mrs. Whorley for interrupting the odious Lord Rockforth's seduction of her.

Chapter Fifteen

It was raining again. Philip glowered at the sky as he took a seat in the moldy-smelling hack. Miserable day, miserable city. It always seemed grey and rainy in London, a manifestation, he thought, of his equally bleak spirits.

He longed for the countryside and sunshine. Not Devon did he envision, but Chipping Campden as he had first seen it, a place of sun on golden stone. *Oolite* he could hear Susan Fairford saying, her hair ablaze with color and curl and light. What would she think of him now that he had left her without a word of explanation?

He could not help comparing her behavior to Lavinia's, her history to his own. Was he deceived in her, as he had been in Lavinia? He had to be sure.

Philip shook off his hat as he stepped inside the smoky, aromatic warmth of the chophouse where he had arranged to meet Mr. Violet, a Bow Street Runner.

Violet was an incongruous name, for not only was he not in the least shrinking, or tender, or pretty, he stank of sausage, ale and sweat. The barrel-chested, mustachioed gent had already secured a table, a steaming jug of coffee and two mugs.

"Chops are on the way, my lord," he said as Philip sank down in the chair opposite. "I took the liberty of ordering."

Philip nodded.

Violet sipped his coffee. Philip poured himself a mug full. The Runner leaned forward to say, low-voiced, "Nasty fellow, this Stott, as you call him—one of many false names he has adopted. Real name, Theodore Stodart, best as I can figure, and your young lady not the first he has taken advantage of."

Their platter of chops and roasted potatoes interrupted him. They fell silent as the serving maid saw to plates, knives and forks. Philip looked about, wondering if Violet had chosen too public a place for their discussion, but the level of noise in the place, a constant din of chattering and clattering, convinced him no one would ever be able to hear their whispered exchange. Violet heaped his plate and fell to carving up his lamb. Philip followed suit.

"There are others?"

"Aye." Violet spoke thickly around a mouthful of food. "My informants have traced Theodore's progress to remote villages north and west of London, each time under a different name. Three other marriages I know of for certain."

"A bigamist?"

Violet washed down his mouthful with a gulp of coffee, wiping greasy lips with a corner of the tablecloth. "No." He shook his head, belched, then went to work with knife and fork again. "Annulled. Errors on the marriage licence."

"He did not use his real name?"

Violet waved a forkful of meat. "That and the bride's age."

"They were not yet twenty-one?"

"Aye, you've guessed it. Needed parental consent they did, every one of them, and did not get it in writing on the licence."

"So many? How has he managed it?" Philip bit into his food without really tasting it.

Violet, who had made short work of what was on his plate, leaned forward to fork another chop. "Devious, he is, your fortune hunter, handsome enough to catch the eyes of the ladies, and well schooled in a charming manner. Seeks out wealthy tradesmen's daughters, the blackguard, young enough that he can fool them, young enough that they can claim forcible marriage to an heiress when he absconds with their assets."

"Is that all he makes off with?"

Violet's jaw stilled, fork halted in midair. His eyes rose from their singular fascination with his food. He chewed and swallowed, biding his time. His answer was carefully framed. He did not pretend to misunderstand. "As to whether he ruined them, my lord, I cannot tell you for a certainty. He left none with child, and two of the young women in question have since found husbands."

Philip nodded, breaking up the potato on his plate with the edge of his fork, watching as it soaked up the grease from the chop. "And the money?"

"Gone, my lord."

"All of it?"

Violet picked up his bone with greasy fingers and gnawed with doglike contentment. "Horses, my lord, stupid punter. He could have retired and lived prettily for the rest of his days on what he has blown on the races."

Susan thought of Philip every day that he was absent. She thought of him at Fairford when she checked in daily to see that the servants did not lolligag about. The house was full of memories of him. It contained, still, a few of his belongings. The stables, too, with Standard to be fed and exercised, were reminiscent of all that had passed between them, good and bad.

She thought of him as she walked the lane and crossed the humpbacked bridge. She thought of him as she stepped through the doorway to her cottage, as she walked the High Street in the direction they had once ridden out of town. She thought of him every time a bee buzzed, or a black-barred dragonfly crossed her path.

They were not all good thoughts.

Who was the woman he went to see about in London? The woman who claimed herself with child, who would bring suit against him for breach of promise? He had been ready to marry her at some point. What had she done to change his mind?

Was Lord Rockforth, like Stott, a fortune hunter? Or something worse? Was he only the victim or was he perhaps the perpetrator? And what was she to him?

The village would not allow her to forget him.

"What has become of your tenant?" the baker's wife asked.

The butcher wanted to know, "How long is Mr. Stone gone? Cook says no more beef deliveries until he returns."

The dairymaid asked the same thing, and the vicar on Sunday.

To each of them she said, "I've no idea."

When she went to pick up her mail, the balding, stoop-shouldered postman, Mr. Peele, said, "Your London *Times* and Bristol *Gazette* have come, Miss Fairford. I see you've listed the leasing of the manor again. Is Mr. Stone to vacate before he has ever gotten good use of the place?"

"He indicated he would not stay above a fortnight," she said.

He shook his head. "No accounting for how some will waste their money, eh?"

Susan flinched inwardly, sure he must find her ridiculous for her own financial losses. She turned to go, but Mr. Peele was not yet finished. "How goes his business in London?"

"I've no idea," she said, tucking the bundle of letters and papers beneath her arm.

It seemed the only thing she said of late.

It was a warm day, and still. She walked through town to the church, its spire poking up out of the huddle of the village's smaller buildings, its fifteenth-century solidity a comfort. She often went to St. James's when she was troubled, to sit by the greying gravestones of her mother and father, to seek a sense of peace, a sense of understanding.

There was a grove of trees there if she sought shade, and a low place in the crumbling wall between the church and the ruins of Sir Baptist Hicks's mansion, where she might sit and contemplate. It seemed fitting she should go there to read her mail, then check the placement of her advertisements and study the listings for governesses and lady's companions.

Was this to be her future? Was it for this purpose she had been well educated and trained in the niceties of societal behavior—that she might trade on it for her own survival?

Her mother and father's tombstones offered no answers, no suggestions, only poignant memories and a growing sense of melancholy.

With a sigh she set aside the papers, and turning, to look over the wall, stared at the squat bulk of the matching Jacobean lodges shouldering the stone gateway to Hicks's property. It was an elaborate flame-finialed arch that led to nothing, had led to nothing since the royalist bonfire that had destroyed Hicks's magnificent house no more than twenty-five years after it was built. All that remained were the twin-peaked roofs of the banquet houses and trees growing where a hall, drawing rooms and bedrooms had once reigned in Italianate elegance.

The Court House, alongside the road, served as a backdrop to the wealth that had once been here. What was left of Baptist Hicks's splendor took up little more space than the almshouses he had built opposite the church.

Kindred spirits, she and Baptist. He had lost much more than she had ever owned. He had gone on with his life. So, too, would she, even if it meant selling Fairford and taking on a position as a lady's companion.

The air smelled sweet—clover and bruised grass. A bee buzzed by her head as she slid from the wall. She wondered if it was one of hers, flown far afield. She thought of Mr. Stone—she must remember to think of him as Lord Rockforth. She wondered what he was doing at that moment.

Philip stepped through the squealing gates, Violet at his heels. The heavy, humid smell of overcooked cabbage, cheap tobacco and urine hung between the damp brick walls, and rose in reeking waves from the slops-stained cobbles. They ducked their heads beneath strings of dripping laundry and stepped around two mongrel dogs rooting through a mound of turnip tops, potato peelings and cabbage leaves.

On either side of them squalid tenements loomed, shutting out sun, and sky and fresh air. More damp laundry dangled limply. Their entrance drew curious looks from the men who idled in the little galleried space that opened up to a patch of sky, from the line of women waiting to fill their pans and buckets, from the barefoot children who ran unwashed and squealing, sticks in hand, after a huge rat.

"That's 'im." The guard pointed a grimed finger. "Still dresses as if 'e 'ad money, that one."

Philip nodded, paid the man, and yet made no move to approach Stott, or Stodart. Now that he had found Miss Fairford's former husband, what had he to say to the fellow? What would he ask? How different were they two, who had both breached their marital commitments? He hoped they were a great deal different, and yet he feared, deep within himself, discovering otherwise.

The gentleman, if one could refer to him as such, was tall, with excellent posture, despite his lowered straits, a proud bearing, and an excellence of dress that declared him the dandy. He wore a once fine hat, carried a carved walking stick with an unusual amber head, and had managed both a well-tied cravat and a high sheen on his shoes, despite the general griminess of his abode. His face was even-featured, with no more than a touch of jadedness in the lines about mouth and eyes. His hair drew back from a high fore-head, thick and dark and straight. His eyes, darker still, were bored in their survey of his surroundings.

He spotted them as strangers as soon as he laid eyes on them and with a slight smile approached.

"Cocky bugger," Violet muttered.

"Reminds me of my brother," Philip said.

"Good day to you, gentlemen," Stodart greeted them. "I cannot recall seeing you here before. What brings you to Ludgate, if I may be so bold?"

"You do," Philip said.

Chapter Sixteen

"Have you heard?" Naomi asked.

On her way home from Fairford, Susan had stepped into Naomi's comfortable cottage for a chat and something cool to drink.

"Heard what?" Susan asked, loosing the fichu from her throat, patting the dew from her forehead with it.

"Warm, isn't it?" Naomi brought to the table a fresh loaf of bread, a knife, butter and a pot of Susan's honey.

"Oppressive. I wish it would rain. It has been promising rain all morning. The roses are begging for it, but the clouds simply sit overhead grumbling. The bees were testy today." She twisted her arm to examine the red spot on the outer edge of her wrist.

"Stung?" Naomi asked.

"Yes. Stupid bee. He gave his life without good reason."

"Oooh. I say, that looks nasty. Is the stinger out? Would you care for some bee balm?"

"Yes, please. It is hot and swollen and bothersome."

Naomi fetched her pot of bee balm salve and kneeling before Susan daubed it onto the red spot.

"He has been sighted in London, you know," she said.

"Who?" Susan knew who, of course, but had to pretend otherwise.

"Mr. Stone." Naomi rose, took up a knife and

plunging it into the bread, said, "He was all the talk at the bakery."

Susan allowed a little huff of exasperation to slip her lips.

Naomi returned to the cupboard for plates and cups. "I know you despise gossip, but thought you should know—"

"But I knew him to be in London. His letter told me as much."

Naomi would not look at her, concentrating on the bread instead as she cut thick, even slices with practiced care. It was a twisted loaf, dense and dark and sprinkled with seed. "Do you care for the heel," Naomi looked up to ask, and for an instant Susan could not decide if she meant the bread or Mr. Stone.

"I prefer a center slice," she said carefully.

Naomi nodded, a twinkle in her eyes. "So do I. Easier to chew."

She carried the breadboard to the table. Susan rose to help. "There is more?" she asked.

"We shall want the cider jug."

"I meant, about Mr. Stone."

Naomi's brows rose. Her lips curved upward. "Interested in gossip? You?"

"I freely admit it. Do not tease me."

Naomi smiled, and then smile fading, said. "No, I shall not tease you. The news is not good. He was seen entering Ludgate, my dear."

"The debtor's prison?" Susan almost dropped the cider jug.

Naomi looked worried as she settled at the table. "There is talk he owes a great deal of money."

"Mr. Stone?" Susan laughed as she sat down to briskly slap butter onto her bread. "I think not. Who dares say such a thing?"

"Joan."

"The silk miller's wife? How would she know anything of Mr. Stone's finances? Has he left a bill unpaid?"

"She was in London visiting her sister, who lives not far from Ludgate. They saw him enter the gates, and being the curious soul that Joan is, the two of them went up to the gatekeeper and asked about the men who had just entered."

"And the gatekeeper said he was a debtor? Preposterous!"

I have urgent business in London.

Urgent debts? Susan's conviction wavered.

A business that may keep me in London indefinitely.

A term in Ludgate might keep a man confined indefinitely—at least until his debts were paid.

A business that cannot be concluded without my participation.

They certainly could not lock someone else up for his debts, had he many. Thoughts flew like startled swifts. Doubt flooded her.

Naomi went on. "The gatekeeper said that if they were referring to Lord Something-or-other and his solicitor, that they had come on a visit, but that any other poor souls who had passed that way were to be pitied, for they owed someone a great deal of money."

Susan's hand shook as she spread honey on her buttered bread. Her voice, she was sure, must give her away as she asked, "Lord Something-or-other? Is that how Joan identified him?"

Naomi shrugged. "No." She unplugged the cider jug's bung, perfuming the air as she poured.

Susan waited on pins and needles to hear more.

"I cannot remember what she said, nor does it concern us. It is not a lord after all that we are speaking of, but Mr. Stone." Naomi looked up to pass Susan's cup. "He is not a lord, is he?"

Susan stared at the film of honey on her bread without really seeing it. What reason had Lord Rockforth to visit someone in Ludgate? "Perhaps an acquaintance is suffering reduced circumstances, and he went to help," she murmured.

Naomi eyed her with increasing interest.

"I am surprised, Susan," she said.

"Surprised?" Susan blinked at her. She was the one surprised.

"You find an unknown gentleman of title more interesting than your Mr. Stone?" Naomi poured a second cup.

"He is not *my* Mr. Stone." In the distance thunder rumbled.

Naomi set down the jug with a thump. The teacups jittered. The knife skittered from the breadboard. "Susan! Do you know more of this than you are telling me? Is Stone this Lord Something-or-other?"

Susan was saved from answering by the freshet of air that stirred the window curtains, by the sudden pelting of rain against the windowpanes.

"Oh, Lord!" Naomi ran to the door, opening it upon the sight of a misty deluge, the closeness of the cottage swiftly cooled by a whirl of rain-scented air. "The lads are out in this. Davey! Henry!" she called into the lane.

"Surely they will have the good sense to seek shelter," Susan said.

"You don't know lads very well." Naomi laughed.

"No," Susan agreed. She did not know lads, of any age, at all.

Chapter Seventeen

Violet threw himself into the hired hack across from Philip, shaking his head and chuckling. The hack, set into rumbling motion, carried them away from the stench of Ludgate.

Three flies buzzed at the glass. Philip let down the window, that they might be freed. The day grew more stifling by the minute. "A wife! Who would have thought the man had a wife he meant to keep?"

Violet, sweating profusely, the rank odor of him filling the confines of the hack, drew a buzz of fresh flies, guffawed and slapped his knee. "Nor that he bloody well insists on taking her with him."

Philip sighed, and eyed the figures that trudged along the streets as they passed, with fresh insight. A knife sharpener whistled as he set blade to the wheel turned by an occasional pumping motion of his foot. A butcher came out of his shop, apron bloody, to feed scraps to two stray dogs. A fellow called out to his monstrous dray horse in a kindly voice. "Come along there now, Bea."

Mention of a Bea, any kind of bee, and Philip thought of Susan Fairford. "Man is a fascinating creature," he said. "Woman vastly more so."

"You fascinate me, my lord," Violet surprised him in saying.

"Me? How so? I was just thinking how very ordinary I find myself compared to most of the individuals that I have encountered of late."

"It impressed me, my lord, how you appealed to the gambler in him, saying he might embark on the biggest gamble of his life if he promised not to return."

"And so it would be, to leave England, and start afresh."

Violet waved a fly away from his nose. "Aye, well enough, but I cannot understand the logic in going to such trouble, my lord. Why do you pay off the debts of that worthless bit of scum?"

"You *will* see to it?"

"Aye. And the passage booked, and papers signed, as you requested."

"You must see them both onto the ship, and the ship out of the harbor?"

"Aye, sir. It shall not sail for America without Stodart and his better half. But why, my lord, do you help such a fellow?"

Philip smiled as he looked out on a city he wished himself away from. "I help myself in helping him."

Violet chuckled. "It is a certainty you help England's unwed daughters."

Philip nodded. *One in particular.*

Everyone in Chipping Campden who liked the buzz of good gossip seemed suddenly in need of a pot of honey. No sooner was the sun up, than bang, bang, bang, Miss Fairford's door knocker sounded.

First, Mrs. Whorley, from next door, stood upon the steps, forehead apucker, hands nervously tugging at her shawl. "Susan, my dear, I hear the most alarming tales. I fear for your safety, my love."

"My safety?"

"It is that horrible Mr. Stone. Does he mean to return?" She lowered her voice as if to reveal something very secret. "I hear he has been thrown into Newgate."

"Ludgate, not Newgate," Susan blurted, and then

regretted having said anything at all, for she must clarify further. "He was not thrown into either, merely spotted entering the place. Do you care to come in, Mrs. Whorley? I have the kettle warming."

"No, no, I will not detain you, my dear. I am on my way to market. But what sort of gentleman frequents prisons of any kind, I ask you?"

Mrs. Whorley was no sooner on her way, than the knocker sounded again and Mrs. Burdock stood at the door, a basket full of empty honey jars in hand. "We are making wheat bread today, Miss Fairford. I require some of your honey, if you please."

"Of course." Susan held wide the door. "Do come in."

Mrs. Burdock trailed after her, jars clinking. "I wonder if you will think me rude in bringing certain news to your attention?"

"News?" Susan asked as she led the way to the larder.

Mrs. Burdock looked about, as if the walls might overhear. "I understand Stone may not be your tenant's name after all," she confided.

"And what would his name be if not Stone, Mrs. Burdock?" Susan calmly fetched down half a dozen of her largest honey crocks.

"Well, I have heard, and from a very reliable source, that our mysterious Mr. Stone is in reality a gentleman of title."

Susan frowned. Thinking of her recent conversation with Naomi, she began to fill the jars.

Mrs. Burdock took a handful of coins from her pocket and counted them out upon the table. "I've no news as to specifics, but that he is a lord, my acquaintance let slip."

And who might your acquaintance be? Susan wondered, spilling honey.

As if she read her mind Mrs. Burdock said, "Someone as should know."

Naomi! Susan did not like to think her dear friend loose-tongued. Had she so soon spread word? The jars filled, Susan wiped up her spill with a damp rag and tried to pry the truth out of Mrs. Burdock as she bent to the task.

The baker's wife proved surprisingly tight-lipped as to her source, however. It took three more visitors, three more secretive warnings against Mr. Stone before the dairymaid revealed the surprising truth as she made her deliveries.

"The banker's wife, in Evesham, enjoys immensely her husband's recent secret connection with an earl, whom she claims resides here in Campden under an assumed name. Can you imagine?"

"The banker's wife?" Susan repeated stupidly.

"Indeed. She crows about it to anyone who will listen. Who can she mean do you think? Could it be your tenant, Mr. Stone? I can think of no other fine gentlemen who have come recently to Campden."

Any answer Susan might have given her was interrupted by the approach of the vicar, who called out as she strode along the street, "Ah, Susan, my dear, I have heard something of your tenant that concerns me."

"Good morning to you, Vicar," Susan said. "You know Marla, the milkmaid, do you not?"

"But of course. Good day to you."

Marla dipped a curtsy and mounted her cart, but she was not yet out of earshot when he said, "A liar, my dear. You house another liar at Fairford, I fear."

She thanked the vicar for his concern and invited him inside. Curtains twitched in Mrs. Whorley's window.

Once inside, a cup of tea heavily laced with honey perched upon the vicar's knee, Susan admitted, "Mr. Stone divulged his true identity to me before departing for London."

"Did he now?" the vicar murmured. "And do you know why the man left in such a hurry?" he asked.

"That I cannot tell you," she said.

As she bid the vicar adieu and showed him out the door, who should ride up but Sir Gregory, in a red-faced state of agitation. Words tumbled angrily from his lips before he had so much as dismounted.

"You will not believe what I have heard, my dear, of the bald-faced liar who sat in my parlor, drinking my tea, while I caught him dead to rights on the matter of his false identity! Knew his father, I did. Met the man, face-to-face. Why in God's name—beggin' your pardon, Vicar—did he not reveal his connection, I ask you?"

"You speak of Mr. Stone?" the vicar surmised.

"Everyone speaks of him," Susan muttered.

"Not Stone. Chalmondeley."

Susan could see the dark shadow at Mrs. Whorley's window, and could only wish the gentlemen might be a little more circumspect.

"I tell you he is up to no good," Wraxall said without heed to the volume of his voice. "There can be no other explanation for such behavior."

Philip stood, hat in hand, at the window in Mr. Dover's office, looking out over the city toward the Thames. The day was warm again, the heat unpleasantly accentuating the stink of the city, the reek of the river. Philip longed for the salty tang of the seaside, for the clovered green of the country. He had left her, given her up, and yet Lavinia still controlled him in keeping him here, unhappy, their business at a stalemate.

"I do not know why Miss Keck should hesitate to agree to the more than generous amount you have stipulated, my lord," Dover complained from his seat at his desk, papers spread before him, his hands nervously twiddling with a dry quill from his engraved

silver inkstand. "But I have never been keen to the
working of women's minds."

"She wants more," Philip said decisively, regarding
the faint ghost of his reflection in the sunlit windowpane. *What do you mean to do about it:* he mentally
asked his pale reflection.

"You have no intentions of obliging her, have you,
my lord?" Dover suggested quietly.

"No," Philip agreed. "I've little inclination to give
her as much as I have already promised. More is out
of the question. But, mark my words, she expected to
enjoy the whole of my fortune, as my wife. She will
attempt to squeeze more out of me."

"How, my lord?"

Philip turned away from the light, the room dark
after so much sunshine.

"I don't know, but she is clever. Even now she
thinks of a way, depend upon it."

"What can we do?"

"Wait for her plan to hatch. It will reveal itself in
a most untimely fashion, I am sure. I do not mean to
kick my heels here in London waiting for it."

"You mean to leave?"

"I do. I return to Chipping Campden tomorrow."

Susan stood at her kitchen window, enjoying the
sunlight. Like a shower it surrounded her, dawn's
communion with God by way of nature. Susan loved
mornings—the cool, dew-drenched sweetness of the
air, the lively twitter and flutter of the birds, the smell
of fresh bread from the bakery when the breeze was
from the east.

This morning she was straining honey, a messy,
sticky task, but when fresh honey had been gathered,
as it had been the day before yesterday, it must be
done. She had not had a spare moment to do so yesterday—too many visitors—too much gossip they
must share.

Today she and the sun had risen together, the house loneliest in the early morning, the village quiet. She thought again about getting a cat. It would be good company.

She hoisted the heavy jars one by one, and allowed them to slowly flow through the strainer, bee wings and dark bits caught in the cloth, honey flowing golden beneath. She ladled the results into the honey pots, each to be tightly sealed with stretched bits of bladder.

In addition, she must cut up the wax hive, that more honey might flow, and finally she melted down the wax itself in a big pot upon the fire, the last of the honey removed to be returned to the bees as food. The wax she poured into candle forms.

It was slow work, the honey thick, reluctant to flow swiftly, perfuming the whole house with a clovered sweetness. Flies were a problem, and the kettle, constantly at the boil—hot water for cleaning the pots, her spoon, the emptied jars and the work surfaces— kept the kitchen humid with steam as she bent over the pot of melted wax. The wisps of hair that escaped the mobcap she used on just such occasions frizzled in limp strands about her face. She turned to the window often, the kiss of the breeze cool upon sweated brow.

When, halfway through the morning the knocker flew against her front door, she muttered to herself, "Who can it be now? The whole village has been here already, have they not?"

She went reluctantly to answer it, wiping sticky hands on sticky apron, knowing she looked unkempt and flushed. It was not a day to be receiving guests. She would simply tell whoever it was to come back later.

But then she opened the door to find a gentleman standing in the deep morning shadows, a gentleman with an all-too-familiar build and posture. For an in-

stant she thought it was Mr. Stone returned, but then
he shifted his weight, and his face withdrew from the
deepest shadow, a face that belonged on Greek statu-
ary, or gracing the body of a plaster angel. Not Mr.
Stone at all, though the green eyes were almost identical, but for a faintly teasing, cocksure light in them.
She had never met such a handsome fellow.

"Miss Fairford?" Even the inflection of his voice
had an attractive ring. "I am told you have leased a
house to my brother."

Philip's brother? The sheer beauty of him was en-
trancing. It made one wish to like this gentleman at
once, for surely something so fair must be good.

Lavinia arrived as he was packing, looking more
beautiful than ever in a demure, round-necked white
walking dress, an azure blue pelisse about her shoulders, the color the perfect foil for eyes a shade deeper
than the fine India muslin.

Her hair, too, was as circumspect as ever, hair the
color of wheat straw in sunlight, neatly wound into a
knot at the crown of her head. She wore the smile she
had always met him with, pearllike teeth gleaming.
One could not tell, looking at her, that she was a
conniving and dishonest wench.

"Philip," she said, and her voice, the same voice
with which she had always called him by his given
name, with exactly the same coy, half-teasing inflection, was that of a stranger. There was no magic there.

Sight of her, however, smote him like blows to
chest, gut and head. He had not seen her since their
wedding day, had not wished to see her ever again.

Queer, he thought, how the ghosts of old emotions
rose when one thought them completely laid to rest.
He had loved her unquestioningly once. Some remnant of that still lived within him, still thrilled at sight
of her, still wanted to welcome her open-armed.

He had never really known this woman, never

known what she was capable of. He ground the wan flame of affection for her beneath the heel of her own betrayal, and responded coolly, "Miss Keck. Forgive me if I do not invite you in, but I am in the midst of packing."

Was it a trace of alarm he saw flit across her features? He had never been good at reading her. He had thought he was, of course. He had believed her face an open book to him once. He knew better now. Miss Keck had guarded her true nature and feelings from him very carefully.

"Packing?" she said. "You mean to leave London? And our business unsettled?"

Another door along the passageway opened. A couple in traveling attire emerged. The gentleman carried two cases. They nodded as they passed and murmured, "Good day," heads bobbing simultaneously, as if the two were one, in some way connected. He had longed for just such connection.

He wished he had never opened the door to find Lavinia before him. The last thing he wanted was to speak to her, to listen to her wheedling.

"I would prefer our solicitors handled our business as you call it, Lavinia. Speaking to each other on the matter can only end in harsh words."

"You underestimate me, Philip," she claimed with a practiced smile. "I am fully prepared to be civil."

"I am not," he said flatly. "And now, if you will excuse me?"

He almost got the door closed before she stopped it with the flat of her hand. "Can we not go somewhere and talk, Philip? After all we once were to each other?"

"I've nothing to say to you, Lavinia, that my solicitor cannot best convey."

She stepped back. "Just like your brother," she said. "You Chalmondeleys are all the same." She turned to go.

He could not close the door on such a taunt. "What do you mean by that?" he asked.

"He has abandoned me," Lavinia told him. "Just as you did."

Philip leaned deep into the leather squabs of the coach he had hired. They smelled faintly of horses and hair pomade. They made a satisfying sound beneath his head, and yet it brought him no comfort. *What to do about Lavinia? How to feel?*

He could not be happy Brett chose to abandon her, abandon the child. Neither did he feel particularly sorry for her. She had made her bed, now she must . . . must what? He placed the flat of his hand against the cool glass of the window, as if to stop the rushed blur of the world as it slid by. Platitudes did not fully encompass his emotion.

He could not determine what she must do. He could decide only what he would do: pay her for his jilting of her on their wedding day, and catch up with Brett.

He must convince him not to leave his child a bastard.

Chapter Eighteen

Susan paused at Naomi's gate later in the day, on her way to the manor to check with the servants, to ensure Philip's brother had made himself comfortable. Her friend knelt in her garden, tending her roses, skirts spread about her as if she, too, bloomed petals.

"Your flowers would seem to enjoy this heat far more than I do," Susan leaned in across the gate to say.

Naomi rose with a glad cry, tucking her garden shears into the basket full of blooms on her arms as she joined Susan at the gate.

"They are particularly handsome this year, are they not?" She proudly pulled a particularly beautiful scarlet rose from the basket and held it to her nose. "I understand you've a handsome new gentleman staying at Fairford."

Susan sighed. "Our Mr. Stone's brother, but I would imagine you have heard by now that the name is not Stone at all."

"I have heard," Naomi admitted, her tone suddenly as prickly as the rose, whose leaves she plucked. "Everyone seems anxious to tell me something of my neighbor, the Earl of Rockforth. Everyone, that is, except you. There is even rumor that he came here straight from a wedding in which he jilted his betrothed."

Feeling as plucked as the rose, Susan inhaled abruptly. "You know more than I do, if the rumor is true."

Naomi returned the stripped rose to her basket and picked up another to denude of its leaves with a brisk efficiency that bordered on callousness. "And what does his brother do here, pray? Can you tell me that?"

"I would not dare to guess, and he has not seen fit to confide in me."

"As you do not see fit to confide in me." Naomi shook the poor rose at her, dew flying from its petals like tears. "I hate to be the last in the village to know what goes on in your life, my dear friend. I feel ever so stupid when news comes to me from the baker's wife or Mrs. Whorley."

"Oh, Naomi!" The hinges of the gate echoed her protest as she leaned toward her friend, hand outstretched. "You know I share more of my private thoughts and feelings with you than with anyone else. The gossip with regard to the Earl of Rockforth stems not from me."

"Who then?" Naomi glared at Susan, then glared at a third flower, as if she meant to frighten it into dropping its leaves.

"I cannot say for certain, but Buttersby handles Rockforth's financial arrangements."

"Buttersby!" Her hands were gentler on the rose. "Oh, my! Foolish man. He must have confided in his wife, who could not keep a secret if her very life depended upon it. I am sorry to have doubted you, my dear!" She thrust forth the flower. "Can you forgive me?"

Susan took it with a smile. "But of course."

"Tell me, then, what think you of Rockforth's brother? What sort of man is he?"

"Charming," Susan said hesitantly, and when Naomi raised her brows questioningly, she elaborated. "Perhaps too charming."

"You do not like him?"

Susan turned the rose slowly, careful of the thorns, regarding it from all sides. She shook her head in frustration. "I do not know him well enough not to like him, and yet—Ow!" she cried out, and dropped the rose.

"Oh, dear," said Naomi. "Found a thorn, have you?"

She found him in the garden, Philip's handsome brother, in nothing but shirtsleeves and breeches, his honey gold hair dappled in sunlight as he stood among the bees, pipe in hand, blowing delicate rings of smoke in the direction of the hive he had opened.

It shocked her to see him standing there, the straw dome in his hand, bees clinging to his shirt, his breeches, his white-stockinged legs. A man in a moving suit of bees, he seemed. They hovered before his face, about his shoulders. They took golden wing from his hair, and yet he stood calm and unstung as he carefully returned the dome to the hive. Foolish and fearless she considered such an act. No one had ever before dared such a thing with her bees. Not even she dared approach them without her netted hat and gloves.

She moved slowly along the walkway, afraid her approach might alarm them. He turned, blowing more smoke from his pipe, the tang of tobacco acrid and masculine, and all too interesting in her garden.

He stepped away from the hives, his gaze upon her, more wisps of smoke trailing from his mouth, from the pipe. With the sun striking the smoke at just such an angle, he seemed engulfed in a golden cloud, something straight out of a fairy tale. The bees fell away from him as he moved. He ignored them, his eyes for her and her alone.

"Miss Fairford," he said as he approached, his voice soft, seductive, as if he meant to bewitch her as readily as he did the bees. He puffed smoke at a bee that still clung to his shirt. It flew away. "Just the woman I wanted to see."

Handsome. Glib. He reminded her of Stott, a memory that stirred a feeling of soured uneasiness—a prickling in every hair upon her scalp. She did not trust Brett Chalmondeley.

"Oh?" She stood waiting, wary of him, of his pull.

"I hope you do not mind my examining your hives?" He waved his pipe at his head. Three more bees took wing.

"Not at all, when it is done so by someone as familiar with their ways as you would seem to be."

"I was surprised to see you have the humane cottage-style hives. Have I any stowaways riding my back?" he asked, turning.

"Yes." Half a dozen still clung to the cloth.

"Will you be so kind as to send them on their way?"

She moved closer. It felt strange, blowing gently on the bees, the fabric of his shirt rippling beneath her breath. One by one, the bees obligingly drifted away.

"There! All gone," she said.

He turned, mouth puckered in a most pleased expression. "And will you blow in my hair, I wonder?" He bent his head that she might look, a cheekiness to his gaze that set her on guard again.

She looked closely, but did not touch, certainly did not blow upon his hair.

His bent head righted itself suddenly so that they faced each other directly. "All gone, are they?"

"Yes."

"Good," he drawled, swaying in her direction.

She backed away a step, wondering how the man managed to make every move, every word, so seductive.

He rifled his hands through his golden curls as she had thought of doing, and as he did, he looked at her so piercingly, his awareness stung. He knew she had considered touching those shining curls.

"I had an apiary of my own once," he said.

"It shows," she said, unable to look at him, choosing

to look at the hives instead. "Did you fume your bees often?"

He nodded. "I prefer to use devil's snuffbox, but in a pinch Kentucky golden leaf will do." He puffed contentedly at his pipe.

"I prefer not to stupefy my bees," she said quietly.

"Oh?" He plucked the pipe from his mouth. "Why?"

"It leaves them too vulnerable."

"Nonsense," he said. "They are short-lived as it is. What harm to the hive if a few are lost so long as it spares one a stinging."

"I wear leno and gloves instead."

"Well." He waved his pipe. "If you prefer, I will not so violate your hives again."

"Thank you," she said, sure she had offended him.

If she had, he hid it well. "As a boy I found the bees vastly intriguing," he said. "In particular, the queen and her completely captivated drones."

Again his words, the look, were suggestive.

Susan turned her back on him, on the angelic lure of his all too dangerous beauty. "We differ again, sir," she said. "It is the workers I value most."

Philip directed the hired coachman to take him first to Evesham. There was business he must attend to.

Mr. Buttersby looked alarmed to see him stride into the bank shortly thereafter.

"My lord!" he squeaked, turning the heads of his clerks.

Philip stopped in his tracks, eyed the clerks as they muttered between themselves in low voices, then linked arms with Buttersby and leaned close to his ear to murmur, "So my secret is out, is it, Mr. Buttersby?"

The menace in his voice succeeded in both liquefying what little backbone the man had, and provoking within him an irritating stammer. "It is, m-m-my lord. I've no idea who m-m-may have let word slip."

"Not you?" Philip drawled irritably as he spun the bank manager in his tracks and with a firm tug propelled him into the privacy of his office.

"I give you my word," the little rabbit stammered. "Is there no one else who knew?"

Only Miss Fairford, Philip thought, and for an instant his heart sank as he sank into the chair in front of Buttersby's cluttered desk. Had she, too, betrayed him?

"Your brother's arrival, did, of course, quash all doubts as to who you are, my lord," Buttersby went on as he settled himself into the creaking depths of his chair.

Philip frowned. "My brother?"

He fell into step beside her, Philip's beguiling brother. "My brother has, perhaps, mentioned me?" he asked, leaning toward her attentively, as if her every move, every word, were vitally important.

"He has not so confided in me," she said.

He chuckled engagingly. "My secrets are safe then."

"Have you secrets, sir?" She sensed hidden truth in his flippancy. Danger lurked in his suave, sophisticated delivery, always balanced on the edge between humor and suggestiveness. He drew and repelled her.

He smiled mischievously, a handsome devil. "We all have secrets, Miss Fairford. Have we not? Has Philip told you his, I wonder?"

She smiled back at him. "They would not be secret then, would they?"

He eyed her a little more keenly. "I wonder, Miss Fairford, have you a honey garden to go with your honey house?" he drawled. "If you have, I should very much like to explore it."

She blushed, uncomfortable with the manner in which he looked her over, head to toe, as he said it, his gaze lingering in a most disconcerting way.

"I have a garden for the bees," she admitted.

He tucked her hand in the crook of his arm as they proceeded, saying, "Philip does not belong here, in your glorious honey house, you know."

She stopped in the pathway. "Whatever do you mean?"

"Well," he murmured, as though the words slipped his lips reluctantly. "If ever there was a drone hanging about his queen it was Philip buzzing about his Lavinia. For years he planned to marry her. He really ought to honor that promise."

Susan had no desire to hear one brother malign the other in his absence. In truth, she had no desire to hear such intimacies of Philip's love for another. She liked him too well. And yet, the entire village had been eager to brand him ill because he was a stranger. They had planted a seed of doubt in what little confidence she had in judging men, especially strangers. Would his brother now fertilize her seedling doubts and fears? Had she been fooled so easily?

"I would not encourage you to speak ill of your brother," she said faintly.

He bent to whisper in her ear. "All of Devon speaks ill of him, I fear, poor Philip. He has, by his own actions, stirred the entire hive of his friends and relations to feelings of disappointment and animosity."

She thought of what the worker bees did to the drones twice a year, when they cast them out of the hive or killed them.

"Small wonder he chose to flee here, to the hinterlands, where no one should know him," Brett Chalmondeley was saying. "No wonder, either, he disguised himself with a false name."

She bent to pinch off papery dead blooms in faded yellow and blue. "Here, as you see, I have planted crocus, and hepatica, which flower early, and there, turnips, mustard and borage, which flower late."

As she rose, she asked, "How has your brother so maligned the world?"

Her voice sounded defensive. She regretted at once the question, regretted doubting Philip, and yet he gave her reason to doubt—her missing Mr. Stone.

It was not her place, or position, to defend a man she knew already to be both liar and philanderer, and yet her heart rebelled against the destruction of her affection, tender bloom that it was. She could not pinch it off as easily as she did the borage. He was the first man she had trusted in any way since Stott had left her—the first man she had in any way opened up to. She did not want her trust again betrayed.

"Ah!" Brett said, regretfully, "he finds a champion in you." He sighed as he broke off a bit of thyme, and lifting it to his nose, breathed deep. "Entrapping yet another fine young woman's good opinion. I will never understand how he manages. Lemon, is it?"

She turned her back on him, focusing her thoughts on her breathing, slowing it. He would lead her into danger. She could sense it. "Of course. And one cannot keep a bee garden without clover and mignionette." She swung her foot at one of the stalky flower heads, scattering petals in a miniature explosion of white.

She waited for the sting of revelation, knowing it was coming, knowing he intended to continue his verbal destructiveness.

"My dear Miss Fairford." He took her arm.

The buzz of his voice offended her, as though from afar. She listened, an unwilling confidant, and he with secrets to tell. "I will not allow it," he said. "I cannot watch another young woman fall prey to his charms."

So sayeth the spider to the fly, she thought.

"He has told you, perhaps, of his engagement to be married?" he asked.

She shook her head. A bee flew past her ear, the buzz raising goose bumps.

"He manages always to attract beautiful, intelligent women."

He patted her arm as much as he meant to pat her ego with such a remark. "Lavinia is a diamond of the first water, her father a baron, her mother distant cousin to the Duke of Cumberland. Everyone thought them desperately in love."

"They were not?" she dared ask, surprised it caused her such pangs to think Philip Chalmondeley in love with another.

"Would a man in love leave his intended on their wedding day, without a word of explanation? I ask you?"

She closed her eyes on the idea of it, stumbling on the flagstones. *He is a jilt as well as a liar!* she thought, *and I am a fool.*

Brett caught her elbow, then braced her by the shoulders. "Are you all right, Miss Fairford? Do I disturb you with such truths?"

He looked and sounded as if he cared, and yet, all she could think or feel was, *Am I deceived again?*

She pulled away from the cling of his hands, of his arm through hers, asking, "She did nothing to earn his wrath? His abandonment of her?"

"Did you?"

"What?" She reeled back, as if he had struck her.

He wore a pitying expression. "I have heard Stott abandoned you the day *after* your wedding."

That he should so baldly state the truth touched a raw nerve.

"You would compare your own brother to such a vile creature?"

Why did she feel compelled to defend Philip Chalmondeley? she wondered. Because he was not there to defend himself?

"Do you know why Philip went to London?" his brother asked.

"Do you?" She turned the question back on him.

"But, of course." His languid assurance surprised

her. Why seek his brother here in Campden if he knew he would not find him?

Brett flung the truth at her like a dagger, his manner nonchalant. "He has gone to consult with his solicitors how best to pay off Lavinia now she is with child."

She refused to be rattled—knowing he meant to rattle her—knowing already about the child. She found his ready tongue contemptible. And yet, she could not stop herself from asking, "Is it his?"

He shrugged. "Who else's? One cannot blame her too much for succumbing to his seduction. Most women of his acquaintance do."

"Seduction?" she scoffed. "The stone-hearted Mr. Stone? You seem far better equipped for such a role. How does your brother go about seducing women? It does not seem at all within his character."

"What? He has not flirted with you, Miss Fairford?"

She shook her head. "He struck me as a man very little interested in women. He carries instead the manner of a man betrayed."

"Ah." He shook his head, pitying her again, and as a result stirring her anger and resentment. She did not like to be pitied. "You see"—he tisked his tongue— "he has begun the seduction, and you do not even realize it. Clever, Philip is, and subtle. I will give him that."

She frowned, her distaste for him intensifying, unconvinced.

"Can you not see it?" he demanded, features mild as he twirled the bit of thyme between his fingers, perfuming the air lemony. "It is so clear to me, who has seen it so many times before. He makes himself mysterious—unapproachable. Women love the challenge. They must unlock the secrets of a man so wounded and tight-lipped."

Doubts assailed her.

"It is not so?" he asked. "Did he not make himself mysterious? Pandora's box?"

Could it be true?

"But I see you are shocked. Do not tell me you have fallen for his ploy? Do not tell me he leaves you in similar condition as his fiancée. Poor girl! Ruined. Who would believe such a circumspect gentleman, after all, seducer of women? He has fooled everyone—his friends, our acquaintances. They would all claim him the more stable of we two. They would more readily believe me the skirt chaser. It is the curse, you see, of this face." He gestured to his flawless physiognomy, as if beauty were something she must pity in him.

She had nothing to say to that.

What she could not understand was why Philip Chalmondeley would not want to claim his own child. Surely he wanted an heir. Why turn the woman away if she carried his future?

"You can imagine the talk it has stirred." Philip's brother liked to hear himself talk, she thought. He liked to flatter her, as well. "I could not let you be similarly deceived."

Was she to thank him? she wondered, too light-headed to do so, too wary.

"And now all of London is astir with the suit she brings against him."

She nodded. She knew, had known. *The baby.*

"Breach of promise." He spelled it out, and she found his willingness to so completely confide in her offensive.

"To call off the wedding is one thing, I'm sure you'd agree, but to leave her pregnant, the babe fatherless!"

"You would talk him into honoring his vows then?" she asked quietly.

"Indeed. What else? And I am wondering, Miss Fairford, if I can convince you to help me."

Chapter Nineteen

She knew he had returned, without word of it ever reaching her. His hired coach went clattering down the High Street that very evening, just as the sun set, shadows gathering. Her heart beat an echo of anticipation and relief. She might talk to him in the morning, discover the truth of the all too lurid flight of rumors that swirled about him like roosting birds.

It never occurred to her she might see him that very night with darkness cloaking her windows. As she readied herself for bed by candlelight, she was startled by a desperate pounding upon the door.

It crossed her mind that it might be he as she stepped into her dress again and fastened ties and buttons on the way down the stairs, calling, "Just a minute!"

What would she do? she wondered, if it was indeed him. Did he mean to pick up where he had left off the evening he had last visited her cottage? He had been about to kiss her then, and she had been about to let him.

It was not he, of course, but Betty, the maid, who stepped in out of the night, breath coming fast, as if she had run there, her face aflush with emotion. "Oooh, Miss Fairford," she moaned. "A dreadful to-do."

"Come in, Betty, come in!" Susan held wide the door. "What is the matter?"

"A great row they are having up at Fairford, miss, Lord Rockforth and his broother. 'Is lordship means to drive Chalmondeley oot of the house, marm, both of them shoutin' and callin' each other names."

"Oh, dear! Have they come to blows? Threatened one another with violence?"

"No, marm, but vile they did speak to one another, and a bit of a scuffle on the stairs. Dented the poor boy's head, they have."

"Whose head?"

"I'm sorry to say they have knocked the shepherd and his dog from the newel post, though it looks as if the whole thing may be reattached given a bit o' carpentry."

"Do you think they have moved on to smashing china? Or stabbing one another with chimney pokers?"

"There is noo telling when men get to fighting, miss. I have quit the place, and noo intention of returning. Me father was a violent man when in his cups. It is best to stay oot of the way when menfolk get themselves in such a state."

"And were either Lord Rockforth or his brother in their cups?"

"Noo, miss. Drunk with anger, they were."

"And could you tell what the fight was about?"

"Could not 'elp but 'ear, miss. 'What are you doing here?' 'is lordship shouts at first sight of 'is brother. 'How dare you take up residence in any place I would call home, after what you did!' 'e says.

"And Brett Chalmondeley's response?" Susan asked, leading the way to the kitchen, where she set a kettle on the fire, and took down cups.

"Do you know, miss, I did begin to like Mr. Chalmondeley a little until I 'eard what 'e 'ad to say to 'is lordship, 'is own brother. 'How could you be so foolish as to think she might love you,' 'e says. And, 'She wanted what I wanted, the money. It is all anyone cares about.'

"We could not 'ear 'is lordship's response in the kitchen, 'is voice is that soft, but 'is brother goes on, words echoing all the way down the stairs.

" 'No?' 'e laughs. 'You care about your reputation, don't you? About the family honor? Ruined,' 'e says, and then something about broken promises and weddin' days.

"They coome closer to the stairs then, and we can 'ear 'is lordship say, 'is voice all cold, and angry, 'And how did you see fit to honor me on my weddin' day, little brother?'

"Mr. Brett laughs then, carefree as you please, and 'e says, all polite, as 'e steps into the stairwell, where every word echoed clear as you please, 'Why, brother, dear, I gave you a most propitious gift. A family heirloom, if you will.'

"That was when 'is lordship shouted, 'Out! Out of this house!' and 'is brother says, 'What, you would cast me from your little honey house? I have seen your sweet Miss Fairford.'

"Their footsteps got quite loud upon the stair then, and the two of them got into a bit of a scuffle, and come a 'orrible rending of wood, then a great crash. Mr. Perry rushed out to see what 'as been damaged. It were 'orrible, Miss Fairford. In all my many years at the manor I have never 'eard such a ruckus."

"There, there now, Betty. The kettle is boiling. Do make yourself some tea. You are welcome to stay the night if you've no wish to return to the manor." Susan threw the shawl on the peg by the door about her shoulders. "I shall not be gone long."

"But where are you gooing, miss?"

Susan swung wide the door, the cool, loamy smell of the night rushing in, the darkness broken by little more than an occasional lamplit window, the glitter of a heaven littered with stars and a whitely glowing crescent of moon. "To see the damage," she said calmly.

The same hired coach, the same four dark horses that had carried Philip to Campden from London passed her in the street, lamps lit, as she walked toward the manor. She raised her hand and almost cried out as it passed, the wind tugging at her cloak, bonnet and hair. It wrenched her heart to think he left again, so soon after he had arrived.

With a cast-off sense of loneliness and unfulfilled yearning, she went on. It was not the broken newel post that drew her into the night. It had been the prospect of seeing Philip Chalmondeley again. Good man, or bad, she cared for him. She had hoped he cared for her enough to tell her to her face what had taken him to London.

The newel post might be mended, but could her heart, now that he was gone, perhaps for good? The house loomed darkly, bright lights moving about on the ground floor, one dimly lit window above.

The front door opened onto a scene of scurrying activity, the servants tidying up the scene of a confrontation, of a hurried exodus, as two traveling bags were carried down the stairs. The air was fraught with tension, the staff as nervous as cats. She greeted the footmen by name, nodded at Perry as he stood leaning on a broom, wood chips at his feet, staring gloomily at the bare wood stump of the newel post, sans its shepherd and sheepdog topper.

"So you've heard of our little fracas?" he asked quietly.

She nodded. "Betty. Can it be repaired?"

"Aye. 'Tis a clean break."

She sighed. "And the boy. Where is he? Betty said his head was damaged?"

"He's taken it upstairs to the red drawing room."

"He?" Hope welled within her like a spring as she caught sight of his hat hooked upon the hall tree, his walking stick in the stand, grey gloves neatly laid ready on the mirrored divider.

"In a foul mood, his lordship is. Asked us to leave him be," Perry warned as she mounted the stairs with a far greater sense of anticipation than was right or proper, or judicious, given what had transpired this evening, given all the negative stories she had heard of him. And yet she could not stop her heart from its expectant pounding, nor slow her steps at the thought of seeing him once again. Perhaps his brother was right, she was seduced by him.

He sat in the dimly lit room, in what had been her father's favorite chair, a leather monstrosity, its back to the door. He sat, shoulders fallen, head bowed, one hand upon the shepherd boy propped in his lap, the other, elbow leaning upon the chair's arms, his fingers steepled across the bridge of his nose.

Her heart welled at sight of the deep, claret-colored leather once again inhabited by a masculine form. The house seemed for an instant whole again, a surprise to her, for she had not realized Fairford fragmented.

She made no sound, and yet he sensed her presence, turning his head as he lowered his hands, the same strong, capable hands with which he had touched her.

"Miss Fairford." He rose, his familiar silhouette blotting the window's light, his shape, his form so pleasing, she longed to run her hands the length of him.

"How happy I am to see you again," he said, his voice as she remembered, deep and gentle, completely captivating. "I have missed you, missed this place. I am sorry to have broken this upon the instant of my return." He held out the shepherd boy, his eyes full of remorse.

Hard to imagine him engaged in a shouting match with his brother, violent enough to rend wood from wood.

"I shall, of course, see to its repair."

"Of course," she said. "And is your business in London concluded? May we expect an extended stay at Fairford this time?" She stopped several steps away from him, hands clasped tightly over her abdomen, as if she would stop herself from moving closer, as if she expected him to pain her there.

"No. Not quite." He sighed. Gently placing the shepherd lad on the floor beside his chair, he gestured to the overstuffed Queen Anne opposite. "Come, sit with me."

She moved carefully to the chair, feeling suddenly clumsy, as if she must trip, or stumble into the chair legs. "I . . ."

"Yes?"

She sank into the well-stuffed comfort she had known since childhood, and waited as he sat again, the creak of old leather all too familiar. She studied his face, his lips, his eyes. All was as she remembered, not as she had been told. Surely this was not the face of a monster.

"I have heard rumors," she began uncertainly, "in your absence."

A stillness possessed him. Nothing moved but his eyes, studying her, and his lips as he said, "Have you indeed?"

"Yes." She did not want to look him in the eyes, and yet she felt she must, that she might divine the truth in them. "They concern you."

His lashes swept down to hide the cool green. "Hardly surprising," he said dryly.

She shifted uncomfortably in the chair. "As I am not given to believing gossip without proof, I would ask you, face-to-face—is it true?"

He leaned back in the chair with a sigh and murmured, "In all likelihood. What have you heard?"

She swallowed hard. "You were to be married?"

"Yes," he said without flinching, his gaze locked unwaveringly on hers, a sadness there, a weariness. She could read no other emotion.

"You jilted her?"

"Yes."

"On your wedding day?"

"I did."

"Did you not love her?"

He closed his eyes and rubbed the bridge of his nose. "Blindly."

That stopped her a moment. He opened his eyes to look at her, delvingly, not at all blind to her reaction.

"She is with child?" The words came out very softly. She longed for a world in which he might deny it was so.

"You know much," he said.

Her voice thinned. "And yet, you refuse to marry her?"

He looked away at last. His jaw worked before he said firmly, "That is correct."

"Have you no conscience, my lord?"

He rose from the chair abruptly, coattails whirling, then walked without speaking to the fireplace, where he plucked up the porcelain shepherdess, lambs bunched about her skirt, and studied it as if a china figurine were more interesting than accusations.

"You think me callous, uncaring?"

She could see his face reflected in the mirror, sadness there. *Pandora's box?*

"You promised to marry her," she said gently. "Yet you would break that promise?"

Carefully, he returned the porcelain to the mantel, then with equal solemnity turned to look her in the eyes. "I would."

"But . . . a man is only as good as his word."

He frowned, lips pressed tightly together, as he crossed to the window, his back to her, as he said, "You judge me harshly. That pains me. I value your opinion." His voice fell. "Above all others."

That he said as much shocked her. Could it be he cared for her, as she had come to care for him? Ill-timed, their emotions. They tempted her to hold silent, and yet all that was good and right and honorable within her cried out to be heard. "You must marry her," she whispered. "You cannot abandon her now . . . in her condition."

He heard her. The deep breath he took let her know that he had, though he did not respond for a long, charged moment as he stared out over the garden.

"You are wrong," he said, voice quiet but firm, implacable. "I will not marry her. You ask too much of me, Miss Fairford."

She rose from the chair and quietly stood watching him, studying the fine figure he cut against the light. She said nothing until he turned to face her, awaiting her answer.

"I thought I knew you, indeed, I had begun to like you, to trust in the goodness in you, my lord, despite the lie of your name. I see now I was mistaken. You are a cipher to me."

"I understand," he began.

She held up a hand to silence him. "You are in need of a housekeeper, sir. I will no longer be able to serve as such. And now I must go."

"Miss Fairford." He meant to stop her.

"No," she said as she moved to the door. "It is late, my lord, and I would go."

Chapter Twenty

As Susan was on her way out, Perry fell into step beside her, saying, "A word, if you will, miss?"

Shaken as she was by her encounter with Philip Chalmondeley, she did not want to deal with household matters at the moment. She did not want to risk the possibility of encountering his lordship again.

"Can it not wait until morning, Mr. Perry?"

"No, miss."

"Something important, Mr. Perry?"

"Indeed, miss. And a matter best not overheard."

Susan sighed. What new household disaster or intrigue would now be revealed? Mr. Perry was a man who knew everything. Quiet, private, discreet, she never saw him gossiping, rarely heard a word of it slip his mouth, and yet, when it was vital to know something about the status of her household, the morale of the staff, who was in a snit with whom, and why, Mr. Perry always came to her. An invaluable trait in him. His confidences had proved timely in the past. She could not deny him now, no matter how out of sorts she was feeling.

"Perhaps you would not mind walking me home, Mr. Perry? The moon offers little light this evening."

"Indeed, marm. I should be happy to oblige."

He brought a lanthorn to light the all too familiar pathway, and made sure they were beyond earshot of the manor windows before he revealed what it was he must tell her, wrapped in the privacy of a small circle of lamplight atop the humpbacked bridge. To the accompaniment of frogs croaking along the stream banks, he said, "I have heard an interesting story from the hired coachman, who brought Lord Rockforth from London."

"Oh?"

"He heard it from the driver who had been hired on occasion to take Lord Rockforth about town while he was in London."

Susan frowned and voiced her displeasure. "You know how I feel about gossip, Mr. Perry. Why did you think I would be keen to hear this?"

"Please hear me out, miss. This concerns you, most particularly."

"Go on."

"Lord Rockforth has, indeed, been to the debtor's prison while in London, in the company of a Bow Street Runner."

"A Bow Street what?" she asked.

"They work with the London constabulary, Miss Fairford. Investigating criminals, I believe."

"And did your coachman informant know *why* Lord Rockforth would deign to enter such an establishment in the company of a constable's informant, Mr. Perry?"

"Yes, miss. Went to visit one of the inmates, he did. A Mr. Stodart."

"A friend of Lord Rockforth's, fallen on hard times?"

"I don't know that they are, or ever were, friends, miss. But, Lord Rockforth saw fit to pay off Stodart's debts."

"How would a coachman know this?"

"Stodart was released, he said. And he and the Runner carried the man, along with his wife, to the docks, where he sailed for America, his passage also paid for by his lordship."

"An interesting story, to be sure, Mr. Perry, but I have yet to see how this directly concerns me?"

"Yes, miss. I never would have troubled you with the tale had the driver not described the gentleman, Stodart."

Susan stared down at the water passing beneath the bridge. A stream full of stars, it seemed, with the darkness in her image blotting the light.

"Someone known to me?" she surmised, a seed of suspicion planted.

He nodded. " 'A fair-haired gent,' the coachman called him. 'Cheeky. He fancied wide lapels,' he said, 'stripey waistcoats and a walking stick with an amber knob, miss.' "

Susan's eyes flew wide. The stars above seemed to whirl, the stars below to tremble. "Amber?" she asked.

He nodded. "There cannot be two such walking sticks in the whole of England."

"How in the world does Rockforth know Stott?" she wondered aloud.

"By way of you, miss. How else?"

"But pay the man's debts? His passage to the colonies? Why?"

Perry fell silent.

"You think Lord Rockforth did this for me?"

"Yes, miss."

"Oh, dear!" she moaned. "I am an abominable judge of character when it comes to men, Mr. Perry."

"Yes, miss."

The following day, a Sunday, with the whole village gathered together under the vaulted fourteenth-century chancel roof of St. James's, the latest gossip could not help but echo nicely, facilitating its spread. This morning's favorite topic was, of course, the all too titillating tale of the Earl of Rockforth, Marquess of Chalmondeley, casting his poor, untitled younger brother, from

Fairford Manor. Handsome, well-mannered young Brett had been forced to put up at the Noel Arms, though Lord knew there were rooms aplenty sitting empty at Fairford.

"A pity that a young man given so much by 'is birthrights, should prove so mean-spirited to 'is 'apless brother," Susan heard the baker's wife say on her way to her pew.

"Small-minded of him, to be sure," Miss Burdock's whispered reply rose high into the windowed nave.

Buzz, buzz, buzz. Like the hum of bees, talk hung as thick as the golden dust motes that swirled lazily before the arched and honeycombed, clerestory windows.

"Did you know . . ."

"Have you heard . . ."

"Is it not dreadful . . ."

"Isn't *he* awful . . ."

All eyes, all heads swiveled in Lord Rockforth's direction at some time before, during or after the service, the buzz fading but not entirely stilled by the vicar's readings from the parable of Job.

Buzz, buzz, the voices swelled, thickening as the choir sang, undiminished when, the service concluded, the church bells ringing, the congregation drifted into the churchyard. Like the dead risen among the leaning rows of tombstones, gossipers clustered along the pathway and between the ball-topped gateposts that led straight into the far more imposing archway to Baptist Hicks's destroyed mansion. With jaundiced discontent, they lingered to observe the exit of "milord," remarking upon how the mighty had fallen.

"He dared to set up house among us," the blacksmith growled.

"A viper in the bosom," the bookkeeper from the Town Hall waxed poetic.

They did not like it, did not like him. He was richer

than they. The rich were not to be trusted, after all,
were they?

He had been dubbed the useless drone. They were
ready to cast him out or kill him. She passed among
them, friends and neighbors—stunned—catching fragments of the fermented brew they made of Rockforth's life.

"I hear there is suit brought against him."

"He leaves a young woman of good family with
child."

"In debt, I understand."

"Purchased passage to the colonies, I am told."

"Would he flee his obligations?"

"What can he have against his brother? Seems a
decent fellow."

"A most ungoverned temper, he has."

"Is it true he has damaged the staircase?"

"Ask Susan, she will know."

They turned to her, avid with interest, in a feeding
frenzy of prattle and idle talk.

She would not be drawn into their tale telling.

Indeed, she turned in the midst of them, stricken,
the words catching in her throat. "For shame! All of
you. That you would come straight from the house of
God to malign a man behind his back. He who has
done nothing but good for the village, in buying your
goods, employing your sons and daughters and paying
for all with good, hard coin."

She surprised them, shocked them, but in no way
shamed them. The dropped jaws and half-open
mouths snapped shut, and then they tried to shame
her instead, turning their tongues to her account.

One murmured archly, "Taken in!"

"Fooled again, poor girl." Burdock shook his head.

The baker's wife tisked her tongue, laughed and
whispered, "Hasn't the sense God gave a green goose,
that one, when it comes to men."

Only one among them took kindly to her defense

of Lord Rockforth, and that was Rockforth himself, who parted them like Moses parting the sea as he stepped from the shadows of the arched doorway.

They fell quiet, watching.

He ignored them, his eyes for her and her alone—those peculiar, cool, treetop green eyes—warming as he looked at her, as he held out his arm in falling into step beside her.

"Will you walk with me, Miss Fairford?" he asked, his every word not loud, but clear and distinct. He meant to be heard.

"I would be happy to, my lord," she said quietly, and slid her hand into the crook of his proffered arm.

They crossed the street in front of the almshouses, aware that they were watched, aware that the talk hummed again in their wake.

She knew it would be said that he seduced her, that he must have taken her to bed to earn such vehement defense. She would be judged a fallen woman before the day was done, the earl's mistress before the sun rose on another Sunday.

She knew the way of it, had suffered much at gossip's hands before, and yet she could not have refused the hand he held out to her.

She savored the silence, the bay leaf–soaped scent of him, the warm solidity of his arm, the nubbed woolen texture of his sleeve.

The High Street unfolded before them, golden, empty, Sunday quiet, the shops closed, a street where past and present met in sublime harmony, Cotswold gables and contemporary cornices cheek by jowl.

"Why do you defend me, knowing what you know?" The cadence and volume of his voice were exactly as she remembered, his breath a warm breeze against her cheek.

"I believe you to be an honorable man," she said, staring at her shoes, at his, in perfect tandem rhythm.

"An honorable liar who abandons the woman he leaves in a family way?" he asked sardonically.

"Honorable at heart, if not in your every action," she corrected him gently.

"Am I?" he asked. "I begin to wonder. My brother would paint a far less charitable picture of me."

"He does not love you like a brother," she dared to suggest.

"No. He has always resented me—my inheritance. One cannot blame him too much."

"Oh? I would. He is despicable to speak of you as he does."

"Our country's system is unfair to younger brothers."

"Life is unfair," she snapped, her voice bitter.

His attention was not wholly fixed on her response. He seemed far more interested, it would seem, in watching a carriage that passed them with a clatter of hoofbeats and a rumbling of wheels on cobblestone.

"Oh, Lord!" he breathed.

"Stop!" A woman's voice issued from the downed window. "Stop the coach!"

The carriage slowed, the horses' heads high. The coachman called to the team, coach springs creaking.

A fair head, ringlets bobbing, leaned from the window. "Philip!"

Beneath his breath, Philip Chalmondeley muttered unhappily, "Medusa."

Releasing the sweet, steadying anchor of her arm, Philip bowed to Miss Fairford, whose gaze passed with calm, almost detached interest from his face to the carriage and back again. "Forgive me—" he began.

"Nonsense!" she interrupted. "Of course you must speak to her."

With an informal tip of the head she set off toward her house, and he, admiring her completely appropriate response, turned to approach the carriage, and in it the woman he least wanted to see in Chipping Campden.

She tapped her fan on the window's metal sash, her gaze following Miss Fairford's receding figure. "What in God's name ever drew you to such an out-of-the-way place? The local beauties?" The lips he had once found attractive twisted with contempt.

"I was not drawn—I fled the ugliness behind me," he reminded her, though it crossed his mind as he, too, regarded Miss Fairford's back, *The local beauty is why I stay.*

Lavinia pouted. "Speaking of ugliness, where is that scapegrace you call a brother. I am told he lingers here."

Philip nodded, eyes narrowing, wondering if she meant to pick up where she had left off with Brett, whether he married her or not. "He does. At the Noel Arms. Do you want him?"

She sighed. "Heaven knows why," she said in the wistful childlike voice that had once enchanted him. "But I do. I have come to convince him he must marry me. And if I cannot, you must do it for me!"

"Does this mean you will drop the suit?"

She smiled sweetly and leaned out of the window to pat his cheek, just as she used to. "You have money, sweet Philip. He has not. And you promised to marry me, which you have not. It was most embarrassing trying to explain your absence on our wedding day."

"*You* were embarrassed? How do you think I felt? To walk in on the two of you? You give whole new depth to the meaning of embarrassed. Tell me, did you mean to continue cuckholding me after the wedding?"

"It is a moot question, Philip, is it not? But you know you must pay for your broken promises, and pay me well, so that the baby your brother hoped would one day inherit the Rockforth fortune as your son may have his piece of it as your nephew."

"That is perverse."

She laughed at him, as if he were a simpleton. "You have never understood how deep runs his anger toward you, have you?"

He stared at her, his once beloved queen bee. He had flown high for her, and then tumbled.

"You know the source of my brother's irrational hatred of me?" he asked.

"But of course," she said, as if it were all too obvious. "You were born first."

While Susan would no longer keep house for Lord Rockforth, neither could she avoid him. The village was too small, and she went often in the vicinity of the manor, to visit Naomi and check upon her bees.

Naomi was busy planning a journey into Devon. Her sister was due for a lying-in, a baby on the way.

"The lads will stay with their father well enough," she said when Susan offered to look after them. "What I am wondering is if you should like to come with me, get away from Chipping Campden for a fortnight?"

"Oh, Naomi! How very kind of you to offer." For an instant the idea appealed greatly, but then Susan thought of the tenant of Fairford Manor, of the impending resolution of his business in Chipping Campden. "However, I must decline."

Naomi smiled. "Too interesting by far, hereabouts, at the moment. Admit it, my dear, you would see how his lordship's sojourn concludes."

Susan blushed, and while she admitted nothing, neither did she deny it.

"You must promise to write me all the news while I am gone," Naomi said as they stood in the doorway talking.

Susan promised, promised as well to look in on the lads and their father. "They will sorely miss their mother's love and care."

"They will miss my cooking, right enough, but as for love . . ." Naomi shook her head. "They are of the age when they do not care for it overmuch."

Susan privately wished she might reach such an age, that she might easily dismiss all longings from her heart. She gave her old nanny and dearest friend a hug, then kissed her on the cheek.

"I shall miss you," she said. "Say hello to your sister and take her this." She tucked a small parcel in Naomi's hands.

"What's this?" Naomi asked.

"Something for the baby," she said, then left without telling Naomi that the swaddling cloth and embroidered linen christening gown had been lifted that morning from swaths of tissue and lavender in her hope chest.

Through the wind-tossed garden she passed, withered rose petals scattered on the path at her feet like lost dreams, and faded heartbreak, pink and scarlet and yellow. She thought of Philip, wishing things were different, the wind sighing for her. Pushed about by the wind, the alders rustled and spoke, tossed leaves like a thousand tongues whispering. What did they gossip about to one another, she wondered? What secrets could they tell?

Hoofbeats intruded on her imaginings as she swung the protesting gate wide. A vehicle, wheels rattling, springs creaking, turned into the lane from the manor. As if her very thoughts drew him, Mr. Stone, no, Lord Rockforth, sat alone beneath the shadowed leather calash hooding his gig.

She waited by the gate, wind tugging at her bonnet, as much as longing tugged at her heartstrings, knowing from the moment he spotted her that he meant to stop. His intent shone in his gaze. It evidenced itself in the movements of his hands as he drew in the reins.

They were strong hands, gentle hands. He had

touched her with them. He had promised them to another.

"Ho, there." His voice moved her, as much as it stopped the horse. "Miss Fairford, I would speak to you."

"You do," she retorted, on her guard with him now more than ever.

"Not here." His gaze turned warily in the direction of the cottage. "Will you come away with me?"

"What?"

"A jaunt in the gig? Outside of the village. Somewhere quiet and private? It is vital we speak."

His need, his voice, sounded too urgent. It frightened her a little. She thought of Stott—how he had lured her into quiet privacy that he might work his wiles on her—that he might convince her she was in love with him. She was convinced already that she cared too much for Philip Chalmondeley, and yet she stepped closer to the gig, eyes narrowed, intrigued by his request, her heart racing like a schoolgirl's. "What of your guests?"

Standard tossed his head, whiffling. Philip soothed him with a word, with a touch of the reins. "My guests, as you call them, stay at the Noel Arms."

She tried to make light of his request, of her own reluctance to answer it. "Can you so little tolerate the company of others?"

"There is one whom I never shun."

He meant her. She could read it in his shadowed eyes. Like the wind, he took her breath away.

He shifted on the seat to make room for her. "They are far happier away from me, let me assure you."

"Are you happy?" she asked, for it seemed to her that sadness lurked in his eyes.

"I am unhappy you should think ill of me, unhappy we have so little opportunity to converse. I did miss our conversations the entire time I was in London."

"Surely a gentleman of standing and position has any number of people willing to converse with him."

He leaned forward, the breeze rifling his hair. Light dappled his cheek and gleamed greenly in his eyes. "Not as you do—as though we are equals, as though you would understand me: mind, heart and soul. No wheedling, no conniving, no false flirtation. You do not clamor. No matter the situation, you remain unrattled, calm, collected, soft-spoken."

His compliments, voiced low, a balm to her soul, drew her. Like the wind in the trees he swayed her.

"You have never meant to win my approval—in fact I believe you did disdain it from the moment we met. And in that way, you have won me completely. My trust, my admiration, my . . ."

Standard tossed his head, snorting. Philip stopped, rubbing whatever it was he meant to say from his lips with the flat of his palm. He sighed and held out his hand.

"Please, I beg of you, come with me."

She could not refuse. Accepting his assistance, she climbed into the sheltered shadow of the gig, settling as a bird settles on a wind-screened branch. As Philip chirruped to the horse, the wheels lurching into motion, the narrowness of the bench threw them together again—hip to hip—a coming home.

Chapter Twenty-one

At a steady trot, Standard carried them out of Chipping Campden into the country, fields stretching on either side, sheep blatting, their bells ringing faintly on the breeze. Lush, emerald green grass and a riot of colorful wildflowers waved in the wind.

They did not notice. Their interests were fixed on each other. He watched the road and the progress of the horse, but only fleetingly, the cool green of his eyes warming whenever he glanced in her direction.

She regarded him steadily, unsure what to make of his request, or her acceptance. The man was trouble. Stott all over again, with a cast-off fiancée, who carried his illegitimate baby. Had she come, as his brother had begged of her, to convince him to do the right thing? She did not try to convince herself it was so. How could she suggest again he marry another and step out of her life forever when he had so firmly refused the first time? When she did not really wish him gone?

"You are wrong," she said at last when the clop of Standard's hooves, like a clock ticking away their time together, went on for longer than she could bear.

His lips thinned. He regarded her, head cocked. "Am I? How so?"

"To think me calm and collected all of the time."

"Oh?"

She nodded, the brim of her bonnet a shield. "Mine

is a carefully constructed facade, like the stone of
Chipping Campden. Hard and golden on the outside,
yet I rub away at the touch, crumbling inwardly."

His hands twitched on the reins. He wet dry lips,
no longer looking at her.

"I must credit the bees," she said. "For teaching
me how to brave the most awkward, trying and fearful
occasions. They sense strong emotion. It stirs them,
and one mustn't stir bees. Your brother has developed
the same calm. We are alike that way."

"You are nothing alike," he bit out, then fell silent,
his anger drifting away on the breeze.

"Perhaps, to bees, strong emotion has a color, a
taste, a smell," she said quietly in an attempt to dis-
charge the awkwardness.

It worked. His hands relaxed on the reins.

"An interesting notion," he said with a smile.
"What color is fear, do you think?"

"Why, yellow, of course," she said.

"As anger is red," he suggested.

She sighed. "And sorrow blue."

"Are you blue, Susan?"

She inhaled abruptly, startled by his use of her given
name, no answer ready. "Whatever makes you ask?"

"When I saw you standing in the lane, the light in
your eyes seemed dimmer than usual today."

"And if I am blue, my lord—"

"Philip."

"If I am blue, Philip, what color are you?"

He sighed, redirecting his gaze at the horse. "Why
I am most certainly grey, for I find myself suffering a
muddy blending of every emotion imaginable: fear,
anger, sorrow, love, joy—all at once. Very wearing."

"Fear, my lord?"

"Yes. I fear I am losing you."

"That would imply you had me."

His head snapped in her direction. He pulled in on

the reins. Standard snorted in alarm. Horse and gig halted in the middle of the empty road.

Turning to look her in the eyes, Philip demanded, "Did I not? Not even a little?" He looked at her, and kept on looking, his gaze delving, the road, the horse forgotten.

"You belong to another," she said, heart aching, unable to continue meeting his gaze.

With a gloved knuckle he raised her chin, insistent. "Do you feel nothing for me? I must know, for I am hopelessly in love, you see."

She could see. Love warmed his eyes and softened his lips. The onslaught of his eyes laid her bare, no chance of hiding her feelings.

He kissed her. She let him. She had yearned for this. Longing for him had gnawed at her soul. In kissing her, he filled the horrible aching hunger within. If only for this instant, the warm bond of their lips made a whole of two halves. Her lips were the flower, and he the bee, seeking nectar. Sweet, this kiss. Dangerous.

Once she gave in to it, she did not want to stop, and in no way could she deny her feelings for him. He tasted of them—honeyed, sweet, golden.

She pushed away at last, head lowered, heart athunder. "This is unwise," she said.

"True," he agreed, breath coming hard and fast, eyes shining. "No place at all for this, the middle of the road. I promised you quiet and privacy, and here we sit where anyone might see. I do apologize."

She chuckled uneasily. "Not the place so much as what we do, my lord."

"Philip," he reminded her.

"Philip," she agreed.

"There is no wisdom in passion," he said. "Has not life taught us that lesson all too well?"

"Yes, but—"

"But," he interrupted, "as lacking in wisdom as our

love may be, it is right—surely you feel that as strongly as I do?"

"I am not so sure."

He frowned, staring at the road ahead, and clucked the horse into motion. Silence settled heavily between them until at last he said, "You are wrong, Miss Fairford."

"Oh?" She noticed he no longer called her Susan.

He nodded emphatically. "Blue cannot be the color of sorrow," he surprised her in saying.

"No?"

He pointed triumphantly to the roadside. "There can be nothing sorrowful or tragic in such a sight, in such a creature, surely."

She leaned forward, confused, for a better view.

Butterflies, big blue ones, a veritable cloud of them, fluttered among the limestone outcroppings.

"Have you ever witnessed a merrier sight?" he asked, directing the gig onto a rutted dirt track that threw them violently against each other. "Come."

He stepped down from the gig, tethering Standard, offering her assistance in alighting with some enthusiasm. "We shall obtain a better view from the rocks, there."

She allowed him to lead her, to help her over rough ground, his hand on hers, on her back, at her elbow.

"They are Cotswold blues," she said.

"And a heavenly, and in no way melancholy, cerulean they are," he said.

Together they made their way up the rocky incline, stepping through knee-deep waves of color: a sea of kidney vetch peaflowers the same shade as her hair, the full-lipped golden horseshoe vetch, matted masses of sunny yellow rock roses. Their passage bruised the aromatic pink wild thyme, the herb perfuming the air, brisk and pungent, an odor somehow fitting, for there was something delicious in their straying from the road. She could taste the potential of the moment, in the beauty of the butterflies, shimmering flickers of iridescent sky on a sea of windswept blossoms. She could feel it in Philip Chalmondeley's touch.

It exploded within, rising through her thighs as her muscles tested the incline, throbbing heatedly in her pulse, her heart aching with awe, with the unparalleled perfection of the moment as they topped the rise, and below them stretched a greater sea of nodding blossoms and winged confetti. An orchard of aging peach trees, gnarled and stubby limbs heavy with golden promise, rode the horizon. Her bonnet strings whipped in the wind. Tendrils of hair flung themselves against her cheeks.

"Sit here," he suggested, "out of the wind."

He took off his coat, the breeze fluttering its tails, fingering his hair, as he spread it on a flat-topped slab of stone that jutted from the hillside like a table. She sank down as he suggested, her heart overflowing with the beauty before her, filled, too, with knowing that he had found at last the promised private place.

He sank down beside her, marveling at the beauty of her profile, copper curls kissing freckled cheek. She was part of the moment, of the flowers and butterflies, of high blue skies, and white, wind-scudded clouds. He marveled that he had convinced her to come with him, convinced her to sit here in the midst of such beautiful nothingness, not a soul for miles.

He ached to kiss her again, for more than kisses between them. Here he had his chance.

"There is a story about the biggest blue butterfly in England," she said.

"Yes?" He leaned on his elbow beside her, admiring the gentle swell of her breast. The only story that truly interested him at the moment was theirs. How would it end, he wondered.

"It is said that its blue-green caterpillar hatches only

on wild thyme or rock roses." She plucked a specimen of each, pink and yellow, and handed them to him.

He could not take his eyes from her lips as she spoke, could not resist touching her hand in taking the flowers.

"These pale blue-green caterpillars are carried away by ants," she said, "when they are very small."

"And do the ants eat them?" he asked, knowing it was not so, and yet wishing her to keep on talking. He sat up to brush a stray strand of coppery hair from the corner of her mouth.

She flinched, blushed a most pleasing rose, and tucked the hair beneath the brim of her bonnet, her fingers drifting to bonnet strings that danced in the breeze.

"No," she said. "It is said the ants feed him their babies—unhatched ones."

He laughed. "Sacrifices to the caterpillar dragon?" He shifted his position, that his shoulder might graze hers, as he tilted his head to regard the butterfly-littered air.

She chuckled. He loved the sound, and turned to look at the amused blue of her eyes.

"That's one way of looking at their symbiotic relationship. I think of them more in terms of drones in the hive."

"Ah. Next you will tell me that the queen of the ants falls in love with this marvelous caterpillar as he fattens on her unborn kin."

She blushed again, fingers playing with her bonnet strings, unconsciously undoing the bow.

"Take it off," he said, his voice husky with desire.

She looked up swiftly, eyes wide.

"The bonnet. Take it off." His mouth had gone dry. "The sight of your hair delights me."

Her lips parted, she inhaled abruptly, breasts rising.

He reached for the strings, for the frozen fingers clutching them.

"Come, let me help."

She exhaled heavily. "I do not think . . ."

"Do not think," he recommended, gently lifting away the bonnet strings, the bonnet rising from the coppery glory of her flattened curls. "Tell me more of fat blue caterpillars gorging on ant queen larvae."

Her eyes, no longer overshadowed by the bonnet brim, shone bluer than the butterflies, emotions fluttering like a flash of wings.

He dared to finger her flattened curls, one by one, fluffing them to life again, releasing their fiery, spiraling glitter. A breathy moan escaped her lips.

He smiled inwardly.

"The ants love not the caterpillar but his essence," she whispered faintly.

He leaned closer to hear. He might have kissed her cheek, her forehead, but he waited, savoring the moment.

"Essence?" he prompted when she seemed to lose both breath and train of thought.

"Yes, they collect a sweet nectar . . ."

With that he must kiss her, his lips brushing her cheek. "From his neck," he murmured, bending to nuzzle her neck, his arms encircling her, pulling her close, that he might explore the length of her spine with searching fingertips.

"Like this?" he murmured, mouth rising along her jawbone, hovering above her lips.

"You knew the story already," she breathed, arching, that small movement all the encouragement he needed to sink his lips to hers.

"Yes," he whispered.

The honey of his kiss was sweeter than any bees might make, his lips first soft on hers, then firm, searching, like the flats of his hands along her spine, into the small of her back.

It was the most natural thing in the world, a beautiful thing, to lie back against the rigid strength of sun-

warmed limestone, his arm pillowing her head, his free
hand drawing her close, his lips everywhere it seemed,
and yet not where she wanted them most, as her body
clamored with aching, heated need for more.

She did not resist when his hand drifted to the curve
of her breasts, when his breath warmed her inner ear,
his tongue caressing its outer shell. She did not protest
when he sank his fingers beneath the neckline of her
bodice, when his fingertips gently circled her aching
nipple. She moaned, arching deeper into his embrace
when he lowered his head, surrounding that still
clothed nipple with the moist heat of his mouth, arousing the ache within her to an excruciating pitch of
wanting, of need.

Above her the sky remained serene, drifting white
on blue, butterflies like shattered fragments of
heaven drifting.

"I want you, Susan," he said, his breath warm
against her neck, hand drifting lazily, tantalizing her
rib cage.

Tears welled in her eyes, overflowing, wetting her
temples. A thin sob caught in her throat. How long
had she waited to hear those words—to feel the rush
again of pure desire?

He shifted, his mouth seeking, his kisses urgent and
tender, his hand still moving, sliding across the sudden
concavity of her abdomen as she drew quick, startled
breath. His fingers drifted lower, grazing fabric, cup-
ping her most private parts through the thickness of
skirt and petticoat, delving fabric, seeking the humid
apex of her desire.

"No!" she cried out, rolling away from his touch,
his mouth, his need. Limestone cut into her back and
the palms of her hands. The wind caught at her hair,
clearing the dense fog of desire from mind, if not
heart.

She shook her head, sought order in her hair and
clutched the strayed bonnet.

He sat up as she planted it awkwardly upon her head, hands shaking. "You do not want me?" he asked, eyes still cloudy with need, his mouth still soft with desire.

Her voice shook. "I . . . I do."

He stilled the frantic movements of her hands as she tucked away her hair. "Let me."

She could not look him in the eyes, watched his hands instead, breathing deep the odor of his skin as he neatly smoothed her hair and tied a careful bow.

"I am a maiden still," she said very softly, her words stilling his fingers. "I would remain so for my husband." She choked on the word. "Should I ever be so fortunate as to find one."

"But . . ." He tilted her chin upward, his green eyes baffled. "Stott?"

She frowned, then pulled away from his touch, fighting the well of fresh tears. "He did not . . . want *me*," she said stiffly, her mouth bitter with the memory of her wedding night. "Only my money, and my horses. He led me—led the entire village—to believe otherwise, of course."

"The fool," he said harshly, tenderly brushing away her tears with his thumb.

She took a deep breath and pressed her lips tightly together, forcing herself to resist the love in his eyes. She rose, butterflies rising with her in a wave of wings. "Come," she said. "You must take me home."

He rose as well, touching her on the shoulder, stopping her retreat. "I must take you home to Devon with me."

Her lips parted. She shook her head, confused.

"I want you in every way, Susan. It was never my intention to dishonor you. Will you do me the honor of becoming Marchioness of Chalmondeley, Countess Rockforth, my wife?"

She blinked at him, startled, and bit her lip. "Are

you free to make me such an offer?" she asked. "Has not this breach of promise suit yet to be settled?"

"I am completely free of heart. What say you?"

She closed her eyes, fearful of all that he offered, convinced it was yet another dream she must wake from. Life had teased her too much with the promise of love for her to leap too wildly, too trustingly again. She wrapped her arms around herself, the intensity of stifled hope painful. "I love you," she said, and when he bent as if to kiss her again, she held her arms rigidly between them, preventing it, saying, "But, I could never marry a man who would abandon"—she stopped, jaw working, her gaze troubled—"who has not made adequate provision for the woman he once loved and a child that is blood of his blood."

She walked away from him then, back straight, posture rigid, nothing butterfly about her.

Chapter Twenty-two

Despite the abrupt harshness of its ending, Philip came away from his stimulating encounter with Miss Susan Fairford, veins burning, as if with too much spirits, stirring him to action, to proof of his undying affections—of his respect for her wishes. His heart was lifted by this irrefutable proof of her feelings, indeed, her desire for him. Hope gave his heart wings. His feet no longer sensibly trod ground.

He wanted nothing less than to take his leave of her, nothing more than to settle the matter of the breach of promise suit with Lavinia with all possible speed.

How could he have believed himself in love before? How close he had come to a marriage of misery, of lies and infidelity. What a stroke of luck it had been to discover himself betrayed. He was, in the current glow of his own happiness, ready to view even Brett, and Lavinia, with some sympathy. Did his brother love Lavinia as he loved Susan Fairford?

He did not think it possible. Their passion was irrefutable given Lavinia's current state of affairs, of course, but was it loving to foist one's beloved into the arms of another—one's own brother? To deny one's own child? It was unconscionable!

How to right this wrong?

Lavinia herself had suggested a solution. He had but to convince Brett he must marry her, must honor the child he had fathered. She seemed ready and willing to agree to such a match as solution, if only Brett might be convinced. Philip knew what Brett wanted: money, title and property. Perhaps if he gave him all three in sufficient quantity, Brett would be agreeable to marriage—Lavinia, too.

And so he sat down at Miss Fairford's secretary on returning to the manor and spent the remainder of the afternoon writing up a list of all of his property that might be deemed unentailed, to which he added generous annual annuities intended for Lavinia and her expected child, following which—with a sense of great accomplishment—he called upon his brother at the Noel Arms, suggesting that they dine together.

Brett evidenced some small surprise in receiving such an invitation, but with an expression of subdued curiosity accepted, further suggesting that the leg of lamb to be had at the Noel Arms was remarkably good.

Lamb was thus called for, and a bit of the local brew, before Brett asked, "And to what do I owe this convivial visit, Philip? Have you decided to marry Lavinia after all? Shall we toast your impending nuptials for the second time?"

"I would much rather toast yours," Philip said, and laid the proposal before his brother while they awaited the arrival of their much touted lamb.

"What's this?" Brett plucked up the pages, peering at them in the candlelight with the assistance of his quizzer. So broad were his gestures, so strident his tone, that the eyes and ears of all who had gathered there turned in their direction.

"It is a list of wedding gifts I am willing to bestow upon you and Lavinia, should you agree to marry her," Philip said quietly.

Brett sat back abruptly, brows raised, blurting out loud enough that he might be overhead, "Surely you jest."

"Not at all," Philip said seriously in the face of his

brother's amusement. "You have only to look at the list to see how serious I am."

Brett threw the pages negligently onto the table. "Nothing you offer interests me, brother."

"But you have yet to read it," Philip protested.

Brett's voice rose a notch. "You would bribe me to marry your fiancée?"

His words carried. Conversation stilled in their immediate surroundings. Curious glances turned their way.

Philip stared at him, astounded and speechless.

Brett was not yet done. He lowered his voice a little, but not enough, contempt evident in his tone, his posture. "I cannot believe you would ask me to assume responsibility for your own issue."

"*My* issue?" Philip said, sotto voce. "You forget yourself, and your culpability."

Brett laughed bitterly, "*Au contraire.* I know myself"—his eyes narrowed—"my place in the world—very well. I know that what you offer me so readily is insufficient."

Again he spoke to the room, and the room listened, a hushed attentiveness stilling the clatter of silver, the clink of glass and plate. They were players on a stage of Brett's making, now Philip's turn to say his lines.

Stunned, but not ready to give up, Philip gathered the pages before him, pushed back from the table, took a gold-plated mechanical pencil from his vest pocket and ceremoniously twisted the casing that the lead might protrude. Knowing he was watched, he scratched through one of the items on the list with a flourish.

"Your ungracious response has cost you that hunting box you always wished was yours. It does nothing to endear you to me, Brett. My generosity, thus abused, will not stand open to you forever."

Every movement carefully unemotional and deliberate, he carefully stacked the pages in the center of the table. "Will you reconsider?"

Brett snatched up the pages, tore them in half with an even greater flourish and thrust them back at him. "It is not enough," he snapped. "Not nearly enough."

"You are a fool. You have no idea what it is you refuse," Philip said temperately, though he boiled with the urge to shake Brett until his teeth rattled. This was not at all the scene he had envisioned in writing up this list.

Their lamb was on the way. A buxom young woman bore it aloft upon a tray, her progress slowed a little by her realization, as she traversed the room, and all eyes turned upon them, that she interrupted something. She came to an uncertain halt when Brett flung the torn pages back at him, a wild and heated gleam in his eyes. "It is not enough, do you hear!" he shouted. "Not for what you would ask of me!"

Baffled, Philip regarded his sibling, a gentleman well dressed and perfectly coiffed, all polish and perfection without, hollow and rotted within.

Would there ever be enough to fill the bottomless depths of Brett's malignant need? "Do you not recognize potential happiness even when it is offered you, Brett, like lamb on a platter?" He spoke loud enough that the neighboring tables might hear his anguish. "Do you even know what it is you truly want?"

"What would you know of wanting?" Brett scoffed, glaring at him. "You, the first born, who has never wanted for anything."

The smell of roasted lamb suddenly offended Philip. The room full of attentive listeners suffocated him. Every word that was said here would be repeated many times over before the morrow dawned.

He pushed back his chair and stood, wordless a moment, loathe to continue airing publicly their lifelong argument. "You and I will always know the truth of this matter, Brett," he said quietly.

"You ask too much of me," Brett still seemed set on telling the world.

Philip obliged him. Speaking louder now, he said plainly, "What I ask of you, brother, is nothing more than that you behave as you would appear to be—a gentleman, accountable for your own actions, your own mistakes."

He turned on his heel and quit the place, knowing that he had accomplished nothing, knowing that the gossips had much to entertain them this evening, at his expense.

The following afternoon, sometime after the latest *on-dits* with regard to Lord Rockforth had made the milk rounds, Miss Lavinia Keck knocked upon Susan Fairford's cottage door.

In opening it, Susan recognized the woman immediately, and thought of poor Philip, who it was said had tried last night to bribe his brother to marry this woman he had loved. He had once admired these pale curls, these blue eyes. How could this foolish female have refused such a love?

Susan knew she could not, had not stopped thinking of it since she and Philip had parted ways. She knew the dreadful gossip she had heard told only half the truth.

"Miss Keck?" she blurted, surprised.

"You know me?" Lavinia Keck's china blue eyes widened in equal astonishment.

Susan allowed herself a smile. "We have few visitors in Chipping Campden. You will find almost everyone in the village knows of your arrival."

"And so I am a source of gossip, am I?" Lavinia asked undismayed, looking up at her from beneath thick lashes, a pretty smile playing about her perfect, bow-shaped lips. A calculated pose by a female accustomed to being the center of attention, one meant to charm. The woman had likely charmed her way throughout her entire life. Susan comprehended how Philip Chalmondeley might have been fascinated by such a woman.

"How may I help you?" she asked, feeling dowdy in her everyday muslin and hand-knitted shawl.

Miss Keck allowed her cool blue eyes to travel slowly from Susan's head to her toes in the most measuring of glances. "Oh, but you have quite a reputation hereabouts, my dear Miss Fairford . . ." She paused suggestively, the shadow of a smile playing about her lips.

"Have I?" Susan refused to be rattled, though she knew Mrs. Whorley to be listening. The woman's shadowy profile hovered on the neighboring window curtain. She had found much to interest her ears of late by way of that window.

Susan took pride in the untroubled calm of her reply. "You must not put too much faith in reputations, Miss Keck. They are not necessarily based on truth."

"Quite right. They are more often rooted in perception than reality," Lavinia said regretfully. "But I have it on good authority you are well known for the sweetness of your"—her pale brows rose—"honey, my dear Miss Fairford. It is Miss, is it not?"

"You wish to purchase honey?" Susan asked with understandable skepticism.

"Indeed. It is on business I come to you."

"Do come in then." Susan held wide the door.

In Miss Keck traipsed, ducking, that her feather-bedecked bonnet might clear the door, her gaze sweeping the interior of the cottage with a trace of dismay. "You once lived in a manor house, did you not?" she asked, her voice so sharply astonished, Susan wondered for an instant if she asked out of sympathy.

"All of my childhood."

"You will understand then, better than anyone, my

reluctance to make a bad match," Lavinia murmured, running her gloved finger along the base of the mantel clock, as if to check for dust.

"Surely no woman sets out to make a bad match," Susan said dryly.

Lavinia walked the length of the front room in three strides. "I cannot imagine how I should ever manage to sustain myself," she said, eyes busy, studying everything in the room but Susan. "You are to be commended for your self-reliance, Miss Fairford."

"How many jars might I interest you in?" Susan asked, wishing the woman gone, wishing her comfortable parlor free from the scorn of one who judged it unworthy with no more than a twitch of her lips and the lift of her beautifully arched brows.

At last, Lavinia turned again her china blue attention in Susan's direction, the flawless perfection of her complexion freshly startling by candlelight. "There is, I must admit, something that interests me more, Miss Fairford, than jars of honey—something that I daresay might prove far more lucrative to you in the long run."

"You have my full attention," Susan said warily.

Miss Keck pursed her lips a moment, another pretty pose. She regarded Susan as if they were old friends. "I wonder if you will tell me how much my fiancé pays you to lease your manor?"

"Why do you ask?"

"Brett tells me you have his brother's ear—his trust, his confidence."

"Perhaps, in some small way."

"I am told you have encouraged Philip to honor his promises to me."

How had she heard that?

Susan waited, more on her guard than ever.

"If this is true"—Lavinia pulled a ribbon-edged reticule from the pocket of her gown, coins clinking—"I should be more than happy to enter into a business agreement with you, in which I shall agree to pay you a twelve-month worth of leases if you will but continue in this fashion."

Susan felt as if the woman had struck her full in the face with the dainty purse. She wanted very much to usher her unwelcome guest out of her modest house at once.

Miss Keck dared to suggest, "If not in keeping with your own sense of honor, then out of sympathy to me, that my child might have a father." One hand absently cradled her abdomen, though it had yet to show any sign of her condition.

Susan felt sick to her stomach. Doubts assailed her. Should she, as this woman suggested, further encourage Lord Rockforth in the honoring of his promises?

"One jar or two?" she asked, voice faint, as she poked her head into the familiar dark and mildly odorous larder. It smelled of aging meat, ripe cheese and yeasty bread. Faintly sweetening the less palatable odors hung the omnipresent perfume of honey—her salvation—her source of sustenance.

"The babe deserves a father," Miss Keck reiterated.

Susan backed out, a single honey pot in hand. "Every child deserves as much," she said.

"You will help me?" Lavinia asked hopefully, eyes sparkling—lovely to behold—charming—a vision of sweetness, and yet Susan did not trust her.

She licked dry lips. "Miss Keck, I am perfectly prepared to do business with you . . ." Lavinia's face took on an avid quality. ". . . with regard to honey. Nothing else."

The bow-shaped mouth pulled tight, the blue eyes sparkled with an unmistakable flash of enmity. "I am disappointed," she said with a pretty pout. "Brett spoke so highly of you. 'A woman of honor,' he called you."

"I wish that I might be similarly kind in describing my impression of Mr. Chalmondeley."

Lavinia had the good grace to bow her pretty head.

"You do not care for him?"

Susan sighed and, crossing to the door, opened it to the breeze, honey in hand. She fingered the seal on the pot, allowing the breeze to kiss her cheeks.

"Do you know the habits of the queen bee, Miss Keck?"

"What has that to do with Brett?"

"No sooner is she hatched, than the queen tears open the cells in which her siblings are maturing, pulls them out, and stings them to death."

Miss Keck's chin rose—a defensive gesture—a trace of obstinance there as she said, "She considers them a threat, of course, potential usurpers to her throne?"

Miss Keck was intelligent, Susan would grant her that much. "Yes," she agreed. "She is quite ruthless in her violence. You see, she does the same to her own children if they would be queens." Susan held out the jar of honey in her hands. "Barbaric, that a female might injure her own babes to maintain a position of power—shameless, and yet we must remember they are only insects and have not our powers of intellect or emotion, no sense of right or wrong. They do not know any better."

"You refuse to help me?" Lavinia surmised.

Susan handed her the honey pot. "My gift to you. I wish you and your babe well, Miss Keck," she said. "I hope you may discover what sustains you and prosper. I even wish you well in regaining Lord Rockforth's waning affections, but I will not help either you or Brett Chalmondeley play queen bee where his lordship is concerned."

Chapter Twenty-three

Philip was not ready to give up. He went, therefore, on the following day to Lavinia with the same list that Brett refused to consider, knowing that suitably motivated she might work her wiles to change his brother's mind.

He was met along the High Street with sidelong glances and open contempt. Word of his confrontation with Brett had spread. Unfriendly whispers followed his progress. The butcher spat as he passed. He was reminded of the day Miss Fairford had defended him in the churchyard. She was not to be seen today, his only weapon against the turn of opinion a stone face and ramrod-straight posture. Lord Rockforth was not at all used to being regarded with such disrespect. It pained him.

The Noel Arms received him no better than the High Street had. The desk clerk sneered openly when Philip asked in which room he might find Miss Lavinia Keck.

"Not in," the young man said. "Shall I leave her a message, sir?"

"Do you have any idea where Miss Keck might be?"

"The lady neglected to inform me, my lord, but she left on foot. Cannot have gone far." The way the lad said it gave the impression he assumed Philip must know far more than he.

"Tell her I called. That I would speak to her."

"Of course, my lord."

Defeated on all fronts, Philip longed for home, for the sea breeze in his face and the taste of salt in the air. Chipping Campden of late proved anything but the golden idyll he had once assumed it to be. His problems followed him. He had not run away from them—simply brought them with him.

As he approached Miss Fairford's cottage, he considered knocking upon the door with a sense of anticipation. She was the only part of Chipping Campden he still treasured. She made his flight from Devon worthwhile—a journey with meaning. And yet she had made clear her wishes. He must resolve his suit with Lavinia.

The door opened, and he looked up with a smile.

Not Susan, but Lavinia, who made her way briskly out of the door, Miss Fairford holding it wide. Their gazes met for an instant, surprised. Lavinia stepped between them, beautiful but angry, cheeks flushed, eyes bright.

"Philip," she said.

His heart sank, though it was she he had been seeking.

"I have just been to the Noel Arms, looking for you," he said, gaze straying, watching with regret as Susan, head lowered, cheek turned to him, quietly closed the door, shutting herself out of their conversation.

"And here I am." Lavinia waved a honey pot. "Sampling the local sweets."

"Will you walk with me?"

His request surprised her. He could see it in the tilt of her head. "What in the world have we to talk about?" she asked, taking his arm as though it belonged to her.

"A settlement," Philip promised. "One I think you will find more than adequate, for yourself and for the baby."

"I am all ears," she said.

He turned their steps toward Shep Street and the river Cam. "What in the world have you two to talk about?" he asked, tilting his head in the direction of Susan's cottage.

She laughed, the sound sweet and clear on the breeze, reminding him why he had fallen in love with her, oh so long ago. "Why what else but you, darling Philip?"

The following morning Philip sat in the window seat of the nursery at Fairford Manor, half turned, that he might look onto the garden—the smell of roses, honeysuckle and dewy grass like balm on the breeze.

He made a habit of taking his morning coffee in this room for several reasons. First, he liked his brew scalding hot. The old nursery was closer to the kitchens than the sitting rooms upstairs. Second, he did not care to occupy the dining room for no more reason than a cup of coffee and toast. And third, perhaps the most important reason, the view and the sweet, bedewed smell of the honeysuckle that grew around the windows pleased him. Morning light slanted at this hour with a particularly pleasing clarity over the flowers and the more distant beehives, Susan's winged charges busy.

This morning the view blurred before his eyes. The coffee lost all taste as he sat thinking of Lavinia and her baby, thinking of Miss Fairford and what he must do.

Susan avoided his company. She no longer came to tend either her bees or the servants. The house rang as empty as his heart without even these fleeting contacts to enjoy. A woman of conviction, Miss Fairford—a woman of honor with high expectations.

Lavinia on the other hand had said she would consider his offer, but she hinted that she was ill inclined to settle for anything less than marriage to a Chalmondeley. It no longer seemed to matter to her overmuch which one. Her reputation was ruined she had wept on his shoulder, and then, just as swiftly as she had sprung tears, she pulled away from him, wiping away her remorse to say, "I can live with that, but that my child, your niece or nephew, should remain a fatherless bastard! It is unthinkable."

She was mistaken. He thought long and hard about it, and did not care for the image. Brett seemed to have no intention of honoring his obligations. He himself had no desire to. Where did that leave the child?

He considered what Susan had said. She claimed she would never marry a man who did not adequately provide for a child, blood of his blood. His niece, his nephew. Could he as callously turn away from this child, as Brett had turned away from their brotherly connection all of his life? He did not like the idea that he wanted to.

And if he did? Could he convince Susan Fairford to change her mind, to marry him despite his warts? He knew he might tempt her, and yet the thought of wheedling, of coaxing her down from her high moral ground revolted him. Would he destroy the forthright strength of character he so admired in bringing her round?

He had promised to marry Lavinia. Right or wrong, he had promised. Did he destroy some vital thread in the moral fabric of his own character in breaching that promise? Especially if it meant leaving a child fatherless?

His coffee cooled, as distasteful and bitter as his thoughts. He leaned forward to pitch the unpalatable liquid into the honeysuckle, knowing with sudden conviction he must leave this place, this honey house, must abandon the sweetest of temptations. He would go home and return to his duties before he became the horrible creature the gossips made him.

He must do his duty by the child Lavinia carried.

*   *   *

Two days later, Susan walked into the bakery on the High Street, into the wonderful smell of cinnamon and raisins and fresh hot bread.

"And good riddance to bad company," the baker's wife was saying. "We hear your tenant means to leave Chipping Campden, Miss Fairford," she called out.

"And none too soon," muttered the squire's maid, who had come to buy the squire's rye.

"You will be glad to see him leave, I'll wager," the baker added his tuppence worth as he came from the back, bearing an aromatic tray full of twisted, poppy seed–dappled loaves.

"Not at all," Susan contradicted. "He was decent and mannerly, and promptly paid me."

"Tore up your stairwell, I hear," he pressed, transferring the loaves to a basket in the display case with a set of tongs.

"And saw to its repair," she reminded him.

"Well, I for one see nothing to miss in him," his wife snapped.

Susan held out a handful of coins, heart aching, her fingers trembling ever so slightly. "Not even his custom? I had heard he was quite fond of your macaroons. I find myself yearning for coconut myself today. A loaf of wheat as well."

Her request and her defense of him, stilled their abuse, but she knew it was only temporary, and walked out the bakery door, the bell jingling in her wake, heavyhearted, despondent and hungry—not for macaroons so much as for some contact with Philip before he left, perhaps forever.

She had seen nothing of him since Miss Keck's strange visit. She had in fact avoided the possibility of contact with him. If he meant to patch things up with Miss Keck, far be it from her to stand in the way. She neglected the hives, and took great care when checking in on Naomi's boys to wait until the lane was clear before traversing it. Otherwise she stayed confined to her cottage, busying herself with cleaning and organization in a place none too disordered to begin with. It saddened her to distance herself thus, and yet she knew not what else to do.

And now he meant to leave!

So troubled was she without Naomi to confide in, that she did as she had always done as a young woman, going to the graves of her parents that she might unburden her heart. She stopped often— stopped that afternoon on the way home from her errands to the bakery and the post office at the Red Lion, where she had been thrilled to find, wonder of wonders, a letter from Naomi.

It was a brilliantly beautiful, sunny afternoon. She had the macaroon and a letter to sweeten the moment, and yet all she saw was the dark progress of her own shadow on the street in front of her. Her mouth was dry, sour. She hungered, but not for macaroons.

She seated herself in her niche on the wall, wished her mother and father a despondent good morning and opened the letter.

Naomi's sister had been safely delivered of a boy, Naomi began. The news should have cheered Susan, and yet it did nothing of the kind. She did, in fact, let slip a tear, wondering if she would ever have children of her own. She dabbed away the moisture, took a deep breath, told herself not to be silly and read on.

Naomi's sister lived in Devon, not far from, none other than, the Chalmondeley estate. The name leapt from the page.

"Can you believe it?" her dear friend went on. "It is a place most impressive."

This she had underlined twice.

"But far more interesting than the property was, of course, the scandal that has so recently rocked it— Lord Rockforth's jilting of Miss Lavinia Keck."

Susan's shoulders sank. She fanned herself with the

letter, wiped a bead of sweat from her temple, then took a bite of the macaroon as she looked out over the sun-drenched estate of Baptist Hicks. One never knew what fortune, or misfortune, the tides of time and change might bring.

This morning had begun with troubling news.

Marla, the milkmaid, had delivered it, along with fresh milk, cream and cheese. "They tell me up at the manor that Lord Rockforth means to return to Devon," the girl had said. "And perhaps better for you that he does. I hear he created a dreadful scene at the Arms."

Susan had said nothing to contradict her. She had heard of the shouting match Philip and Brett had engaged in. Everyone seemed bent on telling her.

There was no more stopping the gossip than her caring for him, no more avoiding mention of him, than the ache in her heart.

She ought to jump down from the wall and walk among the tombstones beneath the shading oaks, birch and alder. The churchyard always gave her a sense of eternity, of mortality, of the brevity of life, and how small her problems really were in the grand scheme of things.

And yet the very warmth of the stones kept her where she was. Heat seeped from the hard mass of limestone through the thin muslin of her dress in such a way that she began to feel a part of the wall, so deeply rooted in Chipping Campden that she would never leave it. The idea was both a comfort and a terror. She turned again to Naomi's letter to avoid thinking too hard on the finality of her union with the wall.

"I dare think you may be interested to hear, despite your aversion to gossip," Naomi wrote, "that it is rumored by those who should know, that on the very morning of his wedding day, Philip Chalmondeley walked in on his affianced in bed with his brother!"

Susan paused with a gasp, eyes wide, horror racing through her veins. *His own brother?* Brett Chalmondeley, who had flirted with her so boldly in the bee garden, hinting at his brother's indiscretion? Who had tried to convince her to help him by way of Lavinia Keck! *The rogue!*

She read on, sitting forward, heels braced against the wall, anxious now to hear gossip as she had never been anxious before, the stone beneath her rump suddenly too hot, too hard, too unforgiving, and yet it mattered not. All that mattered were the harsh words before her.

"The child Lavinia carries"—Naomi's handwriting was not easy to decipher, and it had been crossed and recrossed in an effort to save on postage—"is said to be a Chalmondeley right enough, just not the brother's whom she would sue for breach of promise." And then, almost indecipherable in the margin in a very cramped hand, "Greedy thing!"

Stunned, Susan stared blankly at the headstones before her, the breeze crackling the page in her hand. Could this be true? Lavinia Keck carried Brett Chalmondeley's child?

"Dear Lord," she whispered. And *she* had had the nerve, the utter gall, to encourage Philip Chalmondeley to honor his promise to such a woman? "Stupid gudgeon!

"What have I done?" she cried out, and leaping from the wall, letter flapping, her skirts held high, she ran as fast as her legs would carry her toward the High Street, toward Fairford Manor, afraid he must be gone, afraid she was too late.

Chapter Twenty-four

The village hummed with activity. The walkways were crowded, the street alive with horses and carts. Market day always drew a crowd of the area's poultry farmers. Pale downy feathers swirled like summer snow on the breeze. Chickens clucked. Roosters crowed. The honking of geese resounded along the High Street, mocking her, slowing her, and she in no mood to be slowed.

She practically ran into Brett Chalmondeley, who stood just beneath one of the gabled arches of Market Hall, talking to a gray-haired old woman with a golden-brown goose under her arm, a bright red kerchief tied about her head. He looked the peacock among barnyard fowl—in his pale blue coat, white breeches and blue, floral-patterned waistcoat.

"Here she is now," he said to the woman as he steadied her with a firm grip. "We have only to ask her if she has had any success in convincing my brother to do the right thing. Miss Fairford?"

He smiled at her sweetly, the flash of his teeth, the practiced curve of his lips raising the hair on the back of Susan's neck. Stott had smiled at her in just such a way. She had believed him charming, as doubtless the woman with the goose found Brett utterly charming. She could see by her expression it was so.

She nodded curtly to the two. She certainly had no desire to speak to such a cur. "Do you mean to buy a goose, Mr. Chalmondeley?" she asked, hoping to skirt the topic he broached so openly in front of strangers.

"I do enjoy cooked goose," he said. "But I was just telling this good woman that you would help me roast a fowl of a different feather."

"Were you?" Susan asked coolly, walking on, knowing her abrupt departure would be noted and commented upon.

As expected, he followed her.

"My brother, you have spoken to him?" he asked.

"Are you in the habit of equating your kin regularly with barnyard birds, sir, in conversations with perfect strangers?" she asked tartly.

"Only Philip," he admitted without remorse.

She did not know how to speak to such a man without her anger besting her, and so she held tongue.

"Indeed, Miss Keck and I are hoping to hear good news of you, Miss Fairford, of the sway you may have had over my strayed rooster of a brother in convincing him to do the right thing."

How could he stand there with a look of lamblike innocence? "The *right thing*?" she spat out, anger rising, anger against Stott, against Brett Chalmondeley, against all men who would so abuse the institutions of love and marriage to their own ends. "Should not the right thing be done by the baby Miss Keck carries, sir?"

"You know my feelings on the matter."

His mild, blameless expression tindered her rage to greater heights. "It was wrong of you, sir, to try to convince me to push your brother into a marriage that can bring him nothing but misery," she said flatly.

It was not at all the answer he expected of her.

"My dear Miss Fairford, I am surprised, indeed, shocked to hear you say so. I was sure you and I were in complete agreement."

"You are wrong."

"You do not think a gentleman should honor his promises?"

"Honor! You speak to me of honor?" How much he reminded her of Stott. Uncanny, that two such men should plague her life.

"Most assuredly," he dared to say. "Do you not agree that it was dishonorable in him to ride away, without a word, on their wedding day?"

"That would depend." Anger simmered in her veins.

"Depend upon what, pray tell?" He dared act shocked.

"On what provoked him to ride away."

Uneasiness flit across his fair features. "You confuse me, Miss Fairford. Was he provoked?"

"You would know the answer better than I."

Doubt clouded his eyes, blighted the self-confident tilt of his head.

"What circumstances would be dire enough, do you think," she toyed with him, "to drive a man from the woman he loved on their wedding day?"

His cocksure facade slipped. "My brother confides in you?"

She shook her head sadly. "He is a private man, and proud, your brother, in no way a gossip. I admire that in him very much."

"As do I," he said, the cocky smile returning.

"There is always gossip, however," she said.

The smile faded. "But I understood you to despise gossip as much as I do."

"Yes. Too much false information to be had," she said evenly.

"My experience entirely," he agreed.

She held up a finger, loathe to have him regain any confidence. "I have found a grain of truth, on occasion, at the heart of most tale telling."

"And what tales reach you of my brother's wedding day that convince you not to take him to task?"

She locked her eyes on his, eager to gauge his reaction. "I have heard that someone close to him . . . a scoundrel he trusted above all others, betrayed him, and that on the morning of his wedding, a day he expected to bring him great happiness, he uncovered that betrayal."

Susan had long dreamed of wiping the arrogant smugness from Stott's face. She took small comfort in chasing it from Brett Chalmondeley's handsome features.

He opened his mouth to speak.

Before he could begin to spout fresh lies, she said quietly, "I have also heard that if the child is to be honored, it ought to be by . . ." She paused.

"By whom?" All color drained from his cheeks.

". . . the father. Do you not agree, sir?"

She left him standing there, wondering how much she knew.

Chapter Twenty-five

She came running across the humpbacked bridge, as if she knew he needed her, as if she knew what her bees had done.

Out of breath, complexion flushed, she was a pretty sight, and welcome, oh so welcome. Philip had missed her greatly these past few days. He did not like to think of leaving her in leaving Chipping Campden, but his business with Lavinia had yet to reach resolution. He could no longer bear to stay where he was so much reviled, yet he could not see his way clear of it.

He was ready to be gone, would have already been on the road south, but for the bees.

"My lord!" she cried, breathless and flustered, eyes gleaming at sight of him, as if she found him as welcome a sight as he did she. "I feared I had missed you, that you must already be gone."

She sounded agitated, as if the idea of their parting troubled her as much as it did him.

"I have just come looking for you, Susan. To tell you I am leaving." He wanted to take her in his arms and kiss her there atop the bridge, the water chuckling beneath them. He wanted to sweep her up and throw her into the coach, insisting she go with him. That was impossible, of course. It would be a grave mistake to toss her into his coach at present. "The lad I sent said there was no answer to his pounding at your door."

There was something else in her eyes. Was it fear? "I was . . . at the church."

"Praying?" he asked. "Is it a sign from God then?"

"A sign, my lord?"

"Philip," he reminded her.

"What sign do you speak of, Philip?" she asked, her mouth curving upward at use of his name.

"Your bees," he said.

Her brow furrowed in confusion.

"The carriage was made ready. I had determined to return to Devon, to do as you suggested in honoring my promises to Miss Keck. Every other avenue I have attempted bears no fruit."

"But—"

It looked as if she meant to grab his arm and refrained.

"I was wrong," she blurted, regret strong in her voice, in her eyes. "You must not go! You must not marry her."

He tilted his head, surprised. *What was this?* Had she changed her mind? "Your bees would seem to agree. They stopped me from leaving."

"My bees? How?"

The carriage, unhorsed, stood waiting in the court-yard, surrounded by a crowd of onlookers. All of the household staff was there and several neighbors. Lavinia Keck, too, well dressed for travel, stood in the manor doorway, as if she could not decide whether she wanted to be inside or out.

Her chin rose when she caught sight of Susan. Her eyes narrowed, as if sight of her was unwelcome, but she was not entirely rude, and so managed a cordial nod.

Even the sight of Lavinia Keck, prepared to embark on a voyage with the man she loved to distraction could not hold Susan's attention, however. The vehicle that was to carry them drew all eyes.

It was an awesome sight. The dark body of the coach moved—more precisely, it crawled—the interior of the coach as well. An undulating mass of bee wings, bee bodies, so many the paint and leather of the carriage was made almost invisible. Their hum, the hum of their wings as the bees on the outside of the swarm fanned those within, joined that of the servants.

"Never seen such a sight!" the scullery maid exclaimed.

"Can you believe it!" Millie Burdock stood open-mouthed, market basket over her arm.

"Whatever made them choose the carriage?" the squire's maid asked.

"Have you ever seen the like?" Philip asked.

"They've swarmed before," Susan said. "Though never in quite so odd a spot. They usually choose a tree on which to cluster. Perhaps they mean to go with you."

"They might prove unwelcome guests before the journey is done," he said. "Lavinia is deathly afraid of bees. Tell me, must my coach become part of your honey house now, Miss Fairford? Or have you some magic to make them vacate peaceably?"

She looked away from the fascinating spectacle to smile at him. "They require a new home. The queen has decided to leave her old household to one of her offspring, and most of the court follows her. Perry and I will offer them something more hospitable than your coach."

The aging butler appeared by the garden gate in that moment, as if her mention of his name was all it took to summon him. "All is ready, Miss Fairford." He held out a bee box, her hat, the leno veil and gloves.

"And how does one coax them into it?" Philip asked.

"Very carefully," she said with a low chuckle, then donned the veil.

*   *   *

His bee bride used a goose quill to bewitch her bees into moving. Encased in flowing white, she approached the buzzing oddity he had once called coach.

Unafraid, she was graceful in the languid steadiness of her step, of the movements of her arms and hands. No sleight of hand here. No false magic tucked up her sleeve. She was real, so very real, as real as the rush of emotion he felt in watching her, in marveling at what she attempted.

"My God!" Lavinia dared come close enough to stand at his elbow. "What madness is this?"

Perry joined them. "She must find the queen," he explained.

"One bee among so many?" Philip asked, alarmed. "But how?"

"The queen has a different shape than the others, and they tend to cluster around her in a ball, guarding her."

"And when she finds the queen?" Lavinia asked, never taking her eyes from the sight of Miss Fairford's advance on the bees.

Perry smiled. "She is the bravest young woman I have ever had the pleasure to serve. An unswerving sense of what must be done. Never fear."

"Good God. They are all over her!" Philip stepped toward her, toward the danger he perceived for her.

Perry caught his arm. "And what would you do then, my lord? Stir them up so that both of you are stung within an inch of your lives? Don't be a fool, man. She knows what she's doing, with bees, at any rate."

They had absorbed her, as much as the carriage. All over the hat they climbed, clustering on the netting, littering her skirt like a living embroidery. They walked her sleeves, and the white feather she carried was covered in them. Slowly, she walked along the side of the coach and leaned in the window; all the while her bee coat grew heavier, thicker, more frightening. She made a slow scooping motion inside the door of the carriage, then her bee-covered arm inched from the window.

And then, as if she had waved a magic wand, the bees began to disappear into the box. In a blur of wings they slid away from the carriage, hovering briefly before the bee box, finding their way inside with a quiet uniformity of direction that seemed unreal, an army of bees in perfect formation.

The canvas top of the carriage reappeared, the hunter's green hammercloth on the driver's bench, the shiny black-lacquered door.

"Amazing," Lavinia breathed.

"Magic!" Philip agreed as they fell away from her hat, her sleeves, the bleached muslin of her dress.

"She is that," Perry agreed. "What a fool the stupid Mr. Stott was. He had no idea that in stealing all that Fairford had to offer he left behind its greatest treasure."

Philip nodded, in complete agreement, acutely aware that he had chosen to be equally stupid.

They all followed her into the garden, except Philip and Miss Keck, who remained where they were, heads bent close, as if they shared secrets.

Susan watched most particularly for Philip, afraid he might step into his carriage and leave now that the obstacle of the bees had been removed.

She could not let that happen, would not allow him to drive away without a word of protest. It took every ounce of her self-control to slowly attach the bee box, by way of a sliding panel, to the new hive Mr. Perry had made ready.

She was too anxious then to remove her gloves and the leno, too careless to look for remaining insects clinging to her hat. One wayward creature lingered on the netting. She made the mistake of trying to push it away with the side of her hand. It stung her on the wrist, where glove and sleeve met, offering no protection.

"Ow!" she cried out, startled.

At once Lord Rockforth was at her side, taking the hat, the netting, the gloves, calling out, "She's been stung."

He led her inside out of the heat and away from the crowd, into the cool, echoing emptiness of the buttery. Miss Keck had the good grace not to follow.

"Does it hurt terribly?" Philip, her dear Philip asked, taking her hand in his, perhaps for the last time, unbuttoning her sleeve and pushing it back. It would have suited her far better had he unbuttoned her elsewhere.

His fingers on her arm numbed her to the sting, reminding her of a different hurt. "Not so much as your leaving," she blurted bitterly, her outburst shocking him. "Not so much as finding out secondhand you meant to go home."

His mouth flew open to respond, but Perry came to them, a familiar vial in hand, and whatever Philip meant to say he closed his mouth upon.

Perry gave the vial to Philip, who dabbed the pungent ammonia spirits on her red and swollen skin.

"And so, another poor worker bee gives up his life for you," he said, his manner, his tone lighthearted, as if he jested with her, and yet his cool green eyes told another story. She could not look away from the sadness she saw there.

"I should not have tried to push him away. I know better," she said.

She spoke to him of more than bees as she looked into those eyes, but dared say nothing more specific with Perry anxiously hovering.

Philip knew there was some added significance to what she said. A puzzled furrow knit his brow.

"A cup of tea, Miss Fairford?" Perry asked.

"That would be lovely. Do you care for tea, as well,

my lord?" she asked. "Or do we keep you from your journey?"

The cool gaze darted away from hers, then back again, as he considered her invitation. "A cup of tea while the horses are put to harness sounds just the thing," he said.

Perry left them.

He still meant to leave, she thought, her wrist stinging fiercely. She had pushed him to it.

He continued to daub at the swollen spot, his touch gentle and soothing and painful all at once. She could not bear to think the gentleness of his hand would never again touch her flesh, that the steady, dispassionate voice might not be hers to hear.

There was nothing dispassionate in the words that burst from her mouth. "I did not know! Can you forgive me? I did not know!"

"Whatever do you mean?"

She was lost in the green of his eyes, in the movement of his lips when he spoke—lost in yearning, in remorse. These had been hers, and she had pushed them away.

"You cannot marry her! You must not marry her," she said, emotion thickening her voice.

He blinked, his expression one of confusion. He put down the rag with which he daubed her wrist, but did not let go of her hand, fingers tensed against the backs of hers, his palm a cradle. "No? Why this sudden change of heart?"

"It was wrong of me to stand in judgment, foolish and bold. I had no idea then, that . . ."

"What?" His fingers tightened on hers.

She sighed. How else to say it but baldly. "I know the child is your brother's."

"Ah."

He let go his hold and turned away—a horrible sensation. She feared she had lost him in delving into his private matters, and yet she had to explain her change of heart.

"I know, too, what you discovered," she said softly, wishing he would turn around, "the morning you were to be wed."

His mouth worked. His brow furrowed. "I am sorry you hear such evil reports of my brother. He is jealous, you know."

"That is no excuse for what he did, what he would do."

"I am not so sure I would not have felt the same had I been second born."

"Felt the same, perhaps, but acted upon it? So viciously? It is not in you."

"I am pleased you should think so. Your opinion has always weighed heavy with me."

Her opinion drove him to leave her, to prove himself a better man than his brother.

"And your betrothed? Can you excuse her actions?"

He made a noise of frustration and turned from the window. "My fault, really," he said.

"Your fault?" She laughed. "How so?"

He smiled ruefully. "I did not know what true love was then." His eyes were bright, warm as he regarded her. "I would ask you something very personal, and hope that you will be forthcoming in your response."

She cocked her head to one side, intrigued. "Yes?"

"Is there . . . any other reason you can think of why I should not marry Lavinia?"

He caught her off guard.

"Any reason at all?"

"I . . ."

"Yes?"

"I could not bear to think I might have encouraged you to live your life unhappily."

He closed his eyes, the slightest frown troubling his brow. "Is that all?"

She sighed.

"I have heard rumor," he said slowly, "that you make a habit of defending my name, my reputation."

"Oh?"

"That you refuse to believe the worst of me when everyone else is completely convinced." He tilted his head to look at her more keenly.

She had no reply other than to look at him, her gaze straying from green eyes to captivating lips and back again.

He bent his head to kiss her, and she lifted her face to his.

"You will remember me?" he asked, voice breaking.

"You still mean to go?" She whispered the words, as if to say them louder made them so.

"The child . . . I cannot cast him from the family."

"Yes." She raised her hand to stop him, heart breaking, her future crumbling. "I know. I understand."

A noise in the doorway diverted their attention. Lavinia stepped into view, her gaze traveling between them with an indefinable emotional intensity. How long had she stood listening?

"Philip," she said sharply, and Susan feared she meant to spirit him away in that instant.

"I leave for London," she said, her voice harsh. "Within the hour, by post coach. Perhaps thence to Paris. I have decided not to return to Devon. There will be too much gossip to bear." Her gaze drifted to Susan, whom she gave a long, measuring stare. "I have decided, as well, that I should not be at all happy married to you. You will send me the money you promised?"

"Of course," he said softly, as if afraid to break a spell.

"Well, then I bid you both adieu." She turned to the door, head high, though her eyes glittered with unshed tears.

"Lavinia," Philip called out to her.

"Yes?" She stopped without turning.

"You will bring my nephew to visit me?"

"The child may be a girl," she said stiffly.

"And I would know her," he said. "If you are amenable."

Her head nodded. "I shall send you word of my whereabouts," she said, then was gone.

Silence welled in her wake, as their stunned disbelief was transformed into mutual joy.

"You will come with me?" Philip asked, eyes sparkling. "To Devon?"

Susan smiled. "You will show me the sea?"

He swept her into his arms and planted kisses on her nose, her cheek, her lips. "Can you be happy leaving Campden behind you?" he asked when at last they stopped to catch their breath.

Fairford Manor? A sudden chill touched Susan's spine. She had not thought that loving him would mean she must give up her home—Naomi.

"We cannot live here," he said. "I am too completely despised. I would not expose a wife"—he smiled, the smile growing—"our children to that."

Arms wrapped about his neck, she cocked her head. "Does this mean you would marry me?"

He swept a bow with her still in his arms, kissing her on the downward sweep. Her head swam. "I do beg your pardon, my love. Have I not made myself clear?"

"Not entirely," she said with a smile.

Taking her bee-stung hand again in his, kissing the swollen red spot on her wrist, he sank to a kneeling position and looked her in the eyes most earnestly. "Will you please marry me, Susan Fairford? Will you come away with me to my home in Devon, leaving all that you know and love behind you?"

She tipped her head, as though considering the matter, dimples peeping. "What if you were not despised?"

"Small chance of that."

"Would you consider keeping Fairford Manor? Spending a few months every year here if you were not reviled?"

He shrugged. "It seems an impossibility, my love, but does this mean you will marry me?"

She smiled and kissed the tip of his nose. "But of course I will. Will you give me a few days in which to make ready."

What could he say, but yes?

Chapter Twenty-six

Susan learned the value of gossip in the next few days, in putting it to good use.

On the following morning she arranged for Naomi's boys, under Perry's supervision, to care for her bees. To Naomi she wrote a long list of instructions, explaining how to take, strain and pot the honey, leaving as well her account books, detailing who bought honey and when.

She gave away as gifts her store of honey in a last "honey run" to the Millers, the Kellys, Nell Blackman and Sir Gregory, adding Mrs. Buttersby in Evesham and the bakery in the High Street to her route.

It was while she visited Mrs. Buttersby's that she let slip a few pertinent details, in strictest confidence, in the story of the Chalmondeley brothers. And it was at the bakery she, quite by accident, dropped her most recent letter from Naomi.

That was all it took.

The letter was soon returned to her of course, and it did not appear to have been perused, but perhaps, after all, the baker's wife had not resisted temptation, for it seemed almost overnight public opinion shifted in Lord Rockforth's favor.

Naomi returned with a plethora of tales to tell about her sister's new baby. She was amazed, and a little put out, to find so much had happened in her absence, but pleased no end to be the very first to learn of Susan's engagement.

*   *   *

They were married at St. James's before they left Chipping Campden, by special licence.

All of the village was there to witness Susan Fairford's second chance at happiness. Many remarked on how clear and steady the bride's voice sounded in repeating the same vows she had uttered once before beneath the ancient, vaulted ceiling.

There was only one blemish to be noted upon the face of the newlywed's joy. The groom's brother did not attend the wedding. Neither did Miss Lavinia Keck, who had left for London, it was rumored, much richer than when she came to Campden.

"Not the groom's babe she carried, but his dreadful brother's," the baker's sister made sure everyone knew. "I have it on very good authority."

Naomi laughed when she heard, for she knew the truth of her letter's little journey, and turned to agree when Sir Gregory was overheard to say, "Is not the bride beautiful? Do you know I knew the groom's father? A capital fellow. A pity he did not live to see his son wed. A pity his brother did not see fit to attend the ceremony either."

"Perhaps not such a shame," the owner of the Noel Arms remarked snidely, "when he is *such* a brother." There were nods and knowing glances exchanged when he went on to reveal that Mr. Brett Chalmondeley ". . . slipped away, like a thief in the night, following the departure of Miss Lavinia Keck."

"Left the place in a mess," his wife said.

The desk clerk was not to be outdone. "And his brother, the earl, was left to honor the bills."

"Speaking of bills"—the baker gave a contented chuckle—"I have never been asked to bake a bigger bride's cake. And a pretty penny I charged for it, you may be sure. The earl never so much as blinked. Who ever thought our Suz would marry such a wealthy gent."

"Of course the earl intends to keep a very healthy account in my husband's bank," Mrs. Buttersby assured everyone. "The countess will want to return to Fairford Manor on occasion."

"And so, we shall be able to claim the marquess and his lovely wife as one of our own for at least part of the year," Timothy Burdock was overheard bragging as the couple were ushered into the earl's crested traveling coach, decorated that very morning by giggling local children with bee orchids, honeywort and honeysuckle.

Lord Rockforth, overhearing him, turned to his new bride as they drove away and complimented her on her insistence that they must be sure to purchase all of the wine and spirits required for their wedding celebration from the Red Lion.

It was not too many days later, and all of them blissful, that saw Lord and Lady Rockforth, arms wrapped about each other, happily standing atop the crest of Hartland Point, Devon, the wind in their faces, the craggy grey cliffs dropping away beneath them in a mist of foam and fog to the sea, which made a constant rushing noise. Above them, gulls rocked, keening, on the wind.

"It is just as you said," Susan murmured, awestruck.

"You like it?" he asked.

"Oh, yes," she said. "It is spectacular!"

He drew from his pocket a bottle that he pressed into her hands.

"What's this?" she asked.

"Something you may find just as amazing." He chuckled. "A wedding gift. From Lavinia, who writes to tell me Brett has followed her to Paris."

"And do you know what is in the bottle?"

He smiled mischievously. "Mead."

"How singularly appropriate." She held the bottle to the silvered light of the sky. "Fermented honey and water. Dare we drink it?" she asked with a playful laugh.

"Do you mind if we do not?" he asked mildly. "I think I should like to make it a keepsake, along with the note that came with it, in my brother's hand."

"What does it say?"

He took a folded page from his pocket and, while she studied the far horizon with a blissful smile, unfolded it to read.

" 'The Teutonians used to drink mead for thirty days after a wedding—their moon of honey.' And it is signed, 'To your honey moon. Brett and Lavinia.' "

"It is a beginning," she said, turning, her hand straying to his cheek. She seemed never to have enough of touching him.

"It is indeed a sweet beginning, my love," he agreed, his eyes for her alone. "But your lips are the only honeyed mead I yearn for at the moment, my dear. I am not quite drunk with you, you know."

And with that he set out to remedy the situation.

For only $3.99 each, they'll make your dreams come true.

LORDS OF MIDNIGHT

A special romance promotion from Signet Books—featuring six of our most popular, award-winning authors...

Lady in White **by Denise Domning**
❑ 0-451-40772-5

The Moon Lord **by Terri Lynn Wilhelm**
❑ 0-451-19896-4

Shades of the Past **by Kathleen Kirkwood**
❑ 0-451-40760-1

LORDS OF LOVE

A Perfect Scoundrel **by Heather Cullman**
❑ 0-451-19952-9

Jack of Hearts **by Marjorie Farrell**
❑ 0-451-19953-7

The Duke's Double **by Anita Mills**
❑ 0-451-19954-5

Prices slightly higher in Canada

Payable in U.S. funds only. No cash/COD accepted. Postage & handling: U.S./CAN. $2.75 for one book, $1.00 for each additional, not to exceed $6.75; Int'l $5.00 for one book, $1.00 each additional. We accept Visa, Amex, MC ($10.00 min.), checks ($15.00 fee for returned checks) and money orders. Call 800-788-6262 or 201-933-9292, fax 201-896-8569; refer to ad # N105 (1/00)

Penguin Putnam Inc. P.O. Box 12289, Dept. B Newark, NJ 07101-5289 Please allow 4-6 weeks for delivery. Foreign and Canadian delivery 6-8 weeks.	Bill my: ❑ Visa ❑ MasterCard ❑ Amex _____(expire Card# _____ Signature _____

<u>Bill to:</u>
Name _____
Address _____ City _____
State/ZIP _____ Daytime Phone # _____
<u>Ship to:</u>
Name _____ Book Total $ _____
Address _____ Applicable Sales Tax $ _____
City _____ Postage & Handling $ _____
State/ZIP _____ Total Amount Due $ _____

This offer subject to change without notice.